Secrets Ghosts and Whispers
Spirit Town Cozy Mystery #2
By Sarah Lewin © 2024

This book is dedicated to:
Authors who inspire a sense of mischief, magic, and mystery
My teachers, parents, and author friends
My four beautiful grown-up children and my amazingly patient husband
And my friends who I have met along my journey
I couldn't have written this without you

Chapter 1

It wasn't the darkness that scared me, but what might be lurking in the shadows. Our normally friendly village shrouded in an atmosphere of mystery as we waited for power to be restored. My mobile firmly in my hand, with the flashlight app ready in case I needed it, my body shook, not with fear, but with the energy of the unknown.

Not normally anxious, the events of the last few days left my nerves raw around the edges. Like cheese grated and left on the kitchen bench, I felt a little off. The nausea built up inside me as the pounding of my heart jarred my body. Could the person fumbling around just outside my door hear it? My fingers reached out trying to locate the umbrella I left somewhere near the front door.

Scenes from a movie flashed in front of my eyes, with one difference. I wasn't a child being terrorised by a couple of bumbling criminals. Newly appointed mayor of Spirit Town, my thirty-ninth birthday only a few weeks away, I'd no intention of letting things in our peaceful village get out of hand again.

A loud bang struck my raw nerves. I remembered I was holding my mobile, the flashlight casting a dubious beam of light as I activated the inbuilt flashlight app.

Get a grip, Beth, I told myself as I straightened up and pulled my shoulders back. I held my mobile in front of my face, which I hoped looked formidable, and yanked open the door.

"Ow! Lower that flashlight!" I would have recognised my best friend's smile, even without my torch. "I'm checking in on you, but it looks like you're doing fine."

"Do you have any more news?" Trepidation crept along my spine. It was late for Seamus to be checking in, even with the increase in petty crime. Thanks to our previous mayor and his fraudulent councillors all getting arrested, we were both new members of the Spirit Town Council. My friend's thick wavy hair hung dishevelled in his eyes. He wiped his forehead, the exhaustion evident in his action. We'd put in long hours over the few days. Were we any closer to figuring out the mystery?

"It's definitely a member of our gifted community causing the anomaly. The electricity company can't repair the issue for hours. Where's the old camp stove? We could make a cuppa while we wait." Seamus was as familiar with the contents of my kitchen cupboards as I was. Best friends since that first day at school so long ago; he spent many afternoons after school with me, in the kitchen, or outside playing. The lit candles on the kitchen bench provided a modicum of light. He bent to search the cupboard under the sink. "I was sure the last time we camped out back we put it under here."

"You realise the last time we camped here would have been more than twenty years ago, right? Mum and Dad probably didn't use it often." A wet, salty tear trickled down my cheek, finding my lip. Their deaths were what had bought me back to my hometown after many years in the big city, pursuing my career as a print journalist. The supernatural portion of the population in our town, and my unique abilities—the thing that drove me away—ended up being the deciding factor in my choice to forgive myself and stay. "They wouldn't have thrown it away though. It'll be around somewhere. Try the cupboard on the back veranda." I handed him my flashlight.

An eerie scream outside sent more shivers up my spine. The hairs on my arms rose, my sixth sense telling me there was someone else in the house. Something brushed against my left shin. I spun around, expecting to see Seamus chuckling behind the torch. He loved a good practical joke. Before I could react, something touched my right leg. Resisting the urge to kick out, I reached my hands out to work out what was going on.

My fingers connected with a tiny furry nose and some whiskers. "Hi, Spark. I thought you were asleep on my bed," I whispered, scooping up the bundle of fur that was my kitten. My heart melted into all kinds of gooey. A couple of months ago, before I agreed to take on the added responsibility of becoming mayor of our village, I'd been gifted with this precious tiny feline.

We bonded immediately. "Did you hear that?" My friend returned, waving the stove in the air. "I found the stove. Better news—the gas bottle appears to have some gas left." He put them on the bench near the kitchen sink.

"I heard the noise. I was about to investigate when Spark came out to check on us. The sound came from out the front."

Seamus and I walked side by side to the front door. He held the torch while I carried my ginger ball of fluff.

I heard a faint crackling noise.

We opened the door, and I gasped as the night sky lit up with fireworks. What concerned me more was the hooded figure who leapt over the front gate and fled down the road.

"The fireworks look brighter with no lights in the town," Seamus commented. I couldn't argue with that. I realised with the absence of the hum of electrical appliances the firecrackers were clearer, crisper and louder too.

"Spirit Town looks pretty tonight. I'm biased though. It's been over two years since I came back, and I love living here more than I imagined."

"You're obliged to say so, now you're our mayor," he joked. "Hey, did you see a figure jump the gate when we came outside?"

"I thought it might have been my eyes seeing things in the shadows. I tend to overreact, and I'm trying to rein in my anxiety." Spark wriggled in my arms. "Let's sit so Spark can wander a little bit. He'll tell us if we need to worry about intruders." I led Seamus over to the wicker setting and eased myself onto a chair. Spark sat quietly while I clicked his lead onto his collar.

Seamus plonked onto the chair beside me. "A coffee would be good about now, and a burger as well."

"Good luck making a burger on that stove." I chuckled. "If you want to make us a cuppa, I'm good here." Neither of us moved as we watched my familiar walk daintily down the four steps to the garden gate.

Not yet six months old, his ginger and white fur was visible as he darted around the geraniums and roses Mum had planted inside the front fence. The aroma of the deep green geranium leaves reminded me of evenings sitting on the verandah with Grandma when I was small. I leant over to smell the dark red petals of the rose bush. As I inhaled, the fragrance transported me back to my childhood, I felt Grandma's presence. A few seconds later my kitten drew me back to the present as he bounded up the steps and into my lap. His tiny paws as clean as he was before, with not a speck of dirt on his body.

"Spark doesn't see a threat anywhere. We must've mistaken a shadow for something more sinister," I mused, absently stroking Spark, whose little paws tickled as he kneaded my legs. Either that, or he wasn't as good a guard kitten as I thought.

"It's been a while since any of our gifted residents played around with their superpowers to this degree. Do you think it's kids, or something more serious?" Spirit Town, little more than a village, was home to an eclectic bunch of people, some of whom had extraordinary abilities. Seamus was referring to my second sight. I had a knack of being able to see what was going on, or who was responsible for incidents that occurred in our town. This was one of a few different 'gifts' I inherited from my mother and her mother before her. I was still getting used to my abilities. Seamus could pull anything apart and put it back together. He could talk to and make friends with anyone. Made him a great negotiator.

"It feels like someone who's experimenting with their skills. Not a teenager, although I think some of the goings on have been teens playing around with their new abilities. I sense there's someone new to town, with a special ability." Spirit Town was considered a haven for people with extraordinary abilities; they lived safely alongside 'normal' residents. I couldn't put my finger on how it worked, or even if our residents fully understood the variety of the population with supernatural abilities in their midst.

"Since our Spirit Festival, we've seen an influx of tourists. A few have chosen to move here permanently. I'm wondering if this is because they have powers. It's not like I can run a poll, asking for numbers of townspeople with unusual abilities and their gifts." People who chose to live in Spirit Town, as a haven, to be just another person with a gift. I wasn't about to ruin that for anyone.

Seamus laughed. "I can't see any way, as mayor or a journalist, you could get away with asking such things. Even now." Another burst of light was accompanied by a crackle as fireworks filled the night sky. "Seriously though, and yes, I know I don't make a habit of being serious, your parents would be so proud of you Beth. You stepped in as mayor, the newspaper is doing well, and you saved the shops in Wynyard Street from being demolished by our greedy, power-hungry former mayor."

"Aw shucks." As the heat rose in my cheeks, I hoped the darkness would hide the rising blush. Three shops in the complex in Wynyard Street had belonged to Mum and Dad. Max, our mayor, attempted to pass an application to knock them down, and build a monstrosity in their place. "I'm curious as to what's happening in our town. Who turned off the power and what else are they going to do? Is it a group of people working together or a solitary troublemaker? What's their motivation?" Spark, chasing a moth between our feet, was unperturbed by the noises. "Spark wouldn't be playing if he thought there any immediate threat. It doesn't feel like any one individual is being targeted." It was difficult to explain my emotions, after the initial shock of the blackout and the strange noises.

"We're not going to answer those questions at midnight." Seamus stifled a yawn, glancing at his mobile. "I'm going home. I'll be back for coffee tomorrow morning. Even if we have to use the camp stove."

"Sounds like a plan." I stood up, Spark following me to the front door, as Seamus disappeared down the steps. I made sure I locked the front doors—wooden and screen. Just in case. I double-checked the back door was bolted, and the windows were closed. Not because of the goings on, it was winter, and we expected a low of zero degrees most nights in June.

A yawn escaped my mouth as Spark snuggled into his usual place on the blanket beside me. His purring, sweeter than any lullaby, would normally send me straight to sleep. Tonight, I couldn't get the image of the intruder out of my head. It was a second sight thing. The tingling skin across the back of my shoulders alerted me that someone or something was lurking nearby. An unwanted presence. What did they want? Did I really see a figure jump the fence? Did they get disoriented with the power failure and come into the wrong yard, realising their error when they heard Seamus and I on the verandah? Maybe that was it. Not necessarily sinister. I took a deep breath in, counting the day's blessings. Since being the sole nominee for mayor of Spirit Town, each day was an adventure. Shop owners had become accustomed to my daily walk around the village. Normally I enjoyed my solitude, and I rarely engaged in small talk. As mayor I found it less onerous than I would have thought, talking to and getting to know the people who lived here.

So why was my sixth sense keeping me awake, when Spark didn't seem concerned?

In that halfway-to-slumber state, a hand rested gently on my arm. The hand familiar, warm. I slowly opened my eyes, thinking I'd dreamt the touch, not expecting anyone would be looking at me. I recognised my grandmother's eyes immediately. She passed away a long time ago, when I was much younger, and I welcomed her regular ghostly visits.

We'd been inseparable, my earliest memories were of this remarkable lady. Grandma taught me everything she knew about plants, nature, rocks, and stones. I was forever on her lap while she read stories, or kneeling by her side, with our hands up to our knuckles in dirt.

Grandma beckoned for me to follow. I walked with her through my bedroom door. Her grey hair piled high into a bun, wearing her long green dress—her favourite one, with the deep pockets handy for filling with rocks, leaves and feathers. On her feet, the old, black worn boots reminded me of splashing in mud puddles in the backyard, shrieking with laughter as we ended up soaked. Mum, her face frowning but her eyes smiling, firmly asked we come in and get changed.

Grandma led me through the front door. Spirit Town looked different. The trees that lined the street were much smaller. Behind the trees, several vacant blocks, overgrown with grass were out of place. Where were the houses? The few houses I saw in the street looked different. Growing up, there was always renovations somewhere along the street. But this, this was before my childhood. The few cars visible in the street, big old Fords and Holdens, confirmed I'd walked into a much earlier version of my hometown. I blinked and squinted as the harsh sun hurt my eyes. Grandma was already a few steps ahead of me. I followed her without a word. People who walked past us nodded or said hello. I responded to each person, although I didn't recognise anyone. A few looked vaguely familiar, but I couldn't put names to the faces.

A group of teenagers were riding their bicycles around an empty lot. The energy was unmistakable, at least one of the teens was gifted. Grandma walked up to a couple of girls who were sitting on the kerb, pretending not to watch the teens. Grandma's face was younger; she was slimmer, and her aura glowed. The girl rose to her feet and led Grandma into the house behind her. One of the boys nodded at his mates, and casually rode over to the same house. He laid his bike against the front step and followed them inside.

What should I do? Follow Grandma? Or head home?

I looked at my clothes for the first time. I was wearing a dress similar to Grandma's. As I debated whether to join Grandma, I heard a noise behind me.

Behind me stood a row of trees. I recognised the Bottom Park instantly, even if the trees were younger. This park existed years before the newer Top Park, popular with families with its fragrant plants and native garden, picnic areas, playgrounds and free barbeques. It was darker and more secluded here, the trees forming a calming canopy, even in this earlier version of itself. I tried to make sense of the whisperings of the trees. Fresh pine needle scents tickled my nostrils. The Christmas trees and the oaks were taller than me, but nowhere near as old as they should be. The eucalyptus aroma wafted on the breeze; I took a deep breath. If this was a dream, I didn't want it to end.

A creature, no larger than my gumboot, climbed down from one of the pinecone trees, beckoning to his friends to follow. Four elves, dressed in faded green shirts and brown corded pants, scurried down the trunk, disappearing behind one of the other trees. I sat crossed legged on the ground, staring at the space where I last saw them, in case they decided to reappear.

My eyelids heavy, I struggled to keep my eyes open. Why did Grandma lead me here? What is it about her past I needed to know? How did this link to what was happening in Spirit Town now? Did we have another mystery to solve so soon after the last? Were there always mysteries to solve in our town and I'd never noticed?

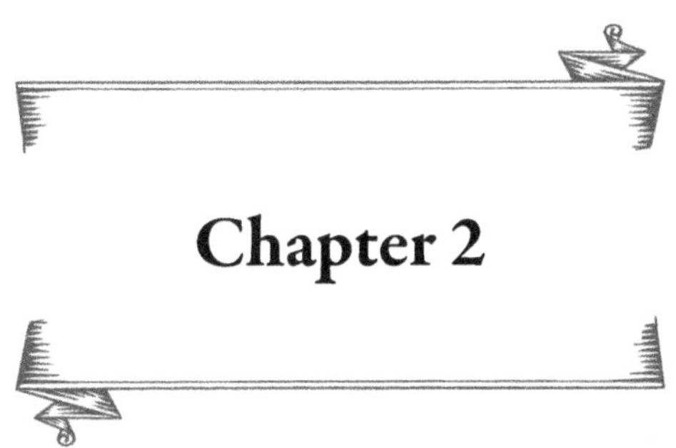

Chapter 2

I awoke to a little sandpapery tongue scratching my hand. "Hey, Spark, cut that out, you know I'm ticklish," I admonished him half-heartedly. It was the best feeling to be woken by my little friend. My alarm clock was flashing 3:45 indicating the power had been restored a couple of hours ago.

The radio announcer relayed some important pieces of information that temporarily wiped away all thoughts of my dream. *During the blackout that enveloped the village of Spirit Town last night, thieves took the opportunity to vandalise a couple of local shops. Police are appealing for anyone who has information about the break-ins, or the whereabouts of the local Police Station sign, to contact the police station. In unrelated news, some farmers have reported missing livestock, so please keep an eye out for and report any wandering farm animals you come across.*

It wasn't the first of April, so this was no innocent practical joke. What would anyone want with the local police sign? It sounded like a prank high school kids would do if dared, or an end of the school year muck up day prank. The shop burglaries didn't sound like kids, at least I hoped not. I guess that depended on what was taken. It seemed unlikely farm animals would disappear or wander off without help. I shook my head to clear the cobwebs. There's no point in getting wound up about it now, this wasn't something I could resolve straight away.

"Come on, little guy, let's check on Buddy." I inherited our pet sheep from my parents, who'd rescued him as a lamb, deciding he would make a great lawn mower. Which he did, once Dad built a series of gates to keep Buddy amused and away from the herbs and vegetables growing in our back garden.

The cool box on the back verandah was stocked with carrots and apples. I picked one of each. Buddy was waiting at the back step. The sheep's teeth crunched through the carrot, polishing off the apple in a few seconds. His cream-coloured wool felt warm, contrasting with the chill in the morning air. The old plastic temperature gauge read two degrees. "Hi Buddy." The words stuck in my throat and came out little more than a squeak. "I know you stay warm in your little lean-to but keep an eye out for any strangers lurking around." Buddy nuzzled my now empty hand. "I'm going inside, for a shower and some warm clothes. I'll visit again later today." Spark was half a step behind me the whole way. I double locked the back door.

As the warm water trickled down my back, flashes of my dream returned. Was it a dream? What else could it have been? Images of olden day Spirit Town filled my vision as I closed my eyes and let the water run over my face. What happened in my dream? What did I learn?

If it wasn't a dream, what was it? Did Grandma take me through a portal to another time? Our village had always been a safe space where people with a variety of magical skills sought asylum—a place where non-gifted people welcomed them, mostly without realising it. If this was more than a dream, and Grandma was trying to pass on some information, what was the message? How was it linked to the events happening in Spirit Town now?

SEAMUS ARRIVED AS I was boiling the kettle for a cup of coffee.

"Do you have an inbuilt radar for caffeine?" I joked.

"Well, yes, and food. I was going to suggest we head to the café. Jon and Lara are going to meet us there."

It didn't surprise me. Earlier in the year, when a series of mysterious incidents threatened our annual festival, the four of us became regulars at *Evie's Café* as we worked through the issues and solved the mystery. Before I became mayor. I missed those catch ups. We shouldn't wait for a crime to solve to get together for a chat.

"Do we need to put up the pet fence, to keep Spark in the kitchen?" Seamus looked around for the wooden playpen I'd been using to get my kitten used to being home alone.

"Spark has the run of the house now. He doesn't jump on furniture, or scratch it, and he always uses his kitty litter. Best trained familiar ever." I gave Spark a cuddle and sat him back on his fluffy grey cushion in the kitchen. It was positioned to get warmth from the heater when it was turned on.

"Could the blackout be the result of an ordinary power failure, do we think teens got carried away with their magic, or worse still it's a deliberate, malicious act?" I asked as I climbed into the passenger seat of Seamus' ute. I normally walked the short distance to the café, but I appreciated the lift, as I pondered my question. I looked out the window, hoping to find the answers to the mystery.

The main street was bustling, which was unusual for this early on a Sunday morning. It reminded me of the events a few months ago, when a bully of a corporation was determined to build a monstrous building in our town. We'd managed to keep the hotel and shopping complex out of our village. Now, people congregated in the street and in the café, as they had then, to discuss the strange goings on. Who could blame them, weren't we doing the same?

"That's the big question." Seamus pulled his old farm ute up around the corner from *Evie's Café*. "The chemist and newsagent were broken into last night. Only a few items taken – all the supplements and a heap of stationery supplies. There's no damage to the buildings. It's as if someone had a key or appeared in each shop, took what they wanted and disappeared. Seamus waved his arm in a grandiose gesture, brandishing an imaginary magic wand. "Magic."

"So, no damage to the buildings, or harm to anyone, just theft of specialised items? Fingers crossed Fred and Jon will be able to capture the thieves. Especially if any of those items stolen end up being sold locally." I couldn't figure out what a thief would need with a range of supplements, not to mention stationery supplies. Was there a black market for health food and school supplies?

Jon and Fred were relatively new to Spirit Town, having arrived a few days before the festival, right in the middle of a crime wave. They were quickly discovering our little village had more than enough incidents to keep the local police occupied. Jon, a little younger than I, tall and thin, with a shaved head and blue eyes, was quick to understand the idiosyncrasies of our spirited town. Fred was younger, with less experience but eager to help, and learn. With mousy brown hair and freckled skin, he was friendly and great with the younger generation. As far as I could tell, neither of them was bestowed with any unusual abilities.

Our residents loved a chat, and I suspected they also loved to solve puzzles and mysteries. We weren't the only people who decided to meet up for a cuppa. The metal chairs outside the bakery were occupied, a few people I didn't know by name, but vaguely recognised, were reading their paper and eating an assortment of pies and pastries. Dad used to love bringing Mum and I here on a Sunday morning. Mum and I would eat lamingtons and meringues while Dad read the Sunday paper or chatted to passersby. I was pleased to see people still enjoyed reading the print edition of the paper.

Toddy from the newsagent had set up a table with the Sunday papers outside the dress shop between the newsagent and the bakery. His shop and the chemist were both still technically crime scenes. Toddy was the same age as my dad, I think they had even gone to school together. "Will Toddy ever retire, do you think?" I asked Seamus. He was much more up to date with what was happening around town, although since becoming mayor I was making myself become more interested. It wasn't that I didn't like people, I didn't always emit friendly *come talk to me* vibes. Unlike my friend, who had a knack of making everyone feel instantly at ease.

"I don't think so. He'd be bored at home. He loves his customers. Even though he's older than a lot of them now, the oldies still stop in for a chat most days. It gives him a reason and a sense of purpose." Seamus's people skills made him the perfect council member. He was as much at home in the gifted community as he was with regular folk.

A few of the oldies were talking to Toddy, so we waved as we walked towards the café. Jon was outside the chemist, talking to Cliff. Around the same age as Toddy, Cliff was a much thinner build. A strong wind would likely knock him off his feet.

Seamus chuckled.

"Darn it! Are you reading my mind again?" I said good naturedly. Ever since our first year at school together, Seamus's ability to read my mind was at the same time annoying and useful. For some reason he couldn't tell what everyone was thinking; such a skill would've been handy in many situations.

"Cliff wouldn't get knocked over in a wind, he'd gently float and land somewhere safe," he replied with a grin.

I watched Lara approach Jon and Cliff. Her honey blonde hair was tied back into a ponytail. Since she arrived in Spirit Town, as owner of the local health food shop, we had become friends. Seamus, Jon, Lara, and I had put our heads together and figured out who was causing the trouble, trying to stop our annual festival. We detoured across the road.

"Do you need a hand with anything, Cliff?" Seamus asked. "Beth and I have a couple of hours to spare."

"Thanks Seamus, Beth." Cliff smiled at us. "Miss Lara here has offered to help. It appears the supplements taken were natural rather than prescription based. No disrespect to you both, but with her knowledge of health food and supplements we'll have the place back to normal and an order placed in no time. I've been trying to convince her to come and work for me." He winked mischievously.

"If I have any of the products at the shop, I'll bring them over for Cliff until his shipment arrives. Whether customers buy here or at the store doesn't matter. As long as they are able to buy the products they need."

"You have a point. We'll bring you both a cuppa and something to eat. After we grab something ourselves," he added.

"That's awfully kind of you, young Seamus." Cliff ruffled my friend's hair, as if we were back in primary school.

I suppressed a smile.

"You can head back inside and start the inventory now, Cliff. Fred will be around later with some follow up questions," Jon said, scribbling in his notepad with a short, stubby pencil. "Does the offer of a cuppa and maybe a sandwich apply to me too?" he asked hopefully. "Now the newsagents and the chemist have been fingerprinted and photographed, I want to double check the cause of the power outage last night. With the lightning strikes and the wind and rain, the technicians were still trying to confirm the source. I doubt I'll make it into the café to join you after all."

"Of course, the offer applies to you." I patted Jon on the arm affectionately. He'd quickly become a valuable member of the community, having been thrown into a crime wave in his first week in the job. I realised I considered him a friend. Before I could work out why my guard was down for the first time in more years than I could count, the town clock struck nine times.

"It feels later than nine in the morning." I suppressed a yawn. "It must be time for coffee."

"At last, you agree with me. Now can we pop into the café? All this talk about food, I'm starving." Seamus grinned.

We opened the door to the café, the little bell signalling more customers for Evie. The constant jangling would drive me mad. I wasn't by nature a patient people-person.

"Ironic, seeing as you are our mayor." Seamus grinned and ducked as I pretended to swipe at him. I wasn't angry he could read my mind. Sometimes it could be annoying, but mostly it was comforting.

It only took a couple of minutes to get to the front of the line. The thing about *Evie's Café*, and the proprietor, Evie, was she was always at work, behind the counter and serving customers with a smile. Behind the scenes in the kitchen, fairies busily cleaned up after each meal, ensuring there was always enough clean crockery and cutlery. Evie's parents, Bessie and Bert, helped by preparing and cooking during the busy periods.

The food was amazing, some called it magic, for no matter what food allergy or intolerance you suffered, you could eat here and never get sick. That's not to say if I ate here every day I wouldn't put on weight, but I never suffered any stomach or dietary related issues. Kids ate free several days a week. Evie's specials were sought after from visitors from the neighbouring towns.

Inside the café we were transported back to a diner from a television show in the Sixties—complete with cosy booths, and red and white chequered tablecloths. In the middle, a high set bench provided a space for businesspeople to enjoy a cuppa or a meal while plugged into the internet. On another wall, a children's corner with miniature furniture, and books and toys were far enough away from the closest booth to give kids independence and their parents a break.

Evie beamed. "What can I get you both this morning? Lucky the power outage didn't last long. Our generator kicked in anyway, so we were fine, but I worried for everyone else without one. Their food could have spoilt if the power remained off for a longer period." Her bright red hair was tied up in a high bun, her blue eyes as friendly and caring as always.

"We're on a mission to get Lara, Cliff, Toddy and Jon some coffees and sandwiches," I said, before Seamus could order.

"After we have coffees and sandwiches ourselves." Seamus quickly interjected.

"How about we organise someone to deliver their food at the same time as you get yours?" She offered.

True to her word, Bessie came to our table with our food at the same time as Bert left the café with a tray of coffees and sandwiches. Evie's sandwiches came with a side of chips, not hot fries, but plain salted chips. I'd ordered ham, cheese, and avocado, toasted. Seamus's sandwich was roast beef and pickles. We ate in silence, which was unusual for my friend. I assumed he was reflecting on the thefts. I sipped my mocha and wondered if the blackout and the thefts were linked.

"What do you have planned for the rest of the day?" Seamus asked, once he polished off his sandwich. I caught him eyeing off the half of my sandwich, sitting innocently on the side of my plate. I pushed the plate towards him. Without any convincing, he picked it up, devouring it as if he hadn't eaten his own a few minutes earlier.

"I know it's Sunday, but would you mind driving past the shops on the way home? I want to make sure they were okay after the power outage." The shops in Wynyard Street were part of my inheritance. Along with the newspaper, my parents had worked hard and renovated the row of five shops, originally built nearly one hundred years ago. Wooden frontage with peaked metal rooves, I'd helped them paint the shops in distinctive pastel colours back when we were in high school.

Seamus made a production of rolling his eyes. "You don't have to work today, Madam Mayor." He grinned, knowing full well it was love and fond memories of my family making me keen to check on the little row of shops. "As I'm choosing to do nothing today, I guess I can spare the time to drive past there on the way up the hill." I did live near the top of a hill in town, not a big hill, but it was good exercise when I chose to walk anywhere.

Being Sunday, only the convenience store was open. I'd forgotten that the seamstress, the laundrette, green grocers and woodworking studio were open six days a week.

"Beth! Hello. The generator out the back worked perfectly last night." Jan came out to greet us as we pulled up in front of the shops. Before I took the mantle of mayor, I'd managed to save these shops from a demolition order. Jan and the others who managed the stores were grateful. "You know your grandma would be proud of you, don't you?" she said softly. "She always insisted you'd do great things, and here you are."

"I'm glad our generator worked, and you didn't lose stock. I'll come back past during the week and say hi to the others. If you have any orange poppyseed cake, I'll grab some then." The urge to hug her was strong, but I wasn't sure how comfortable she would be. As I was enveloped in a bony armed embrace, I understood it was her feelings I had picked up on.

"You could always pick up cake today too," Seamus suggested.

"I have a banana cake for you, young Quinn. If I am not mistaken, it used to be your favourite."

"I won't say no." Seamus said as we followed Jan into the shop.

Jan refused Seamus' money. "You've turned out okay, young man. Your family would be proud, too."

I watched my friend blush, one of the only times I had witnessed him lost for words. As tempted as I was to tease him, I decided against it.

"Do you mind if we call back past to see how Toddy and Cliff are coping?" Seamus reverently placed the banana cake on the seat between us in the front of his ute.

"I don't mind at all." I stopped as my phone beeped. I read the text, typing a response as I filled Seamus in. "Lexi, checking to see if she needed to come into work today. I told her to stay home and enjoy her weekend." Although my only employee at the paper was indispensable, she worked long enough hours during the week.

My phone beeped again. "Izzie, asking how we are faring, after the blackout." I answered my old school friend and reporter at the local radio station that all was okay.

"Thanks for coming back to check on the oldies." Seamus pulled his ute into a space right outside the chemist. "Dad would want me to make sure they were fine." Seamus' parents had left their businesses, which included two farms, a saddlery and a fishing tackle shop, to their only son. After forty-five years of hard work, they decided to take ten years off and travel around the world in a yacht. "Italy," Seamus answered my unasked question.

"Dad was at school with them, played basketball with them, and even played in a band with them, a long time ago." Seamus didn't talk much about his family, or their gifts. I never asked for details, I'd spent far too long trying to ignore the gifted residents, in particular, the fact that I belonged to that portion of our population.

Leaving Seamus out the front of *Toddy's Newsagents*, I caught a glimpse of Lara through the chemist window. I circled around to the other side of the street, to one of the newest businesses, *The Magic Shop*. The window showcased some of what the non-magical folk thought of when they heard the word *magic*. Packs of playing cards, red hearts and diamonds, black clubs and spades, lined up next to a pair of dice and some colourful scarves. A fluffy, white toy rabbit sat propped up in a shiny, black top hat. Open on Sundays, the store was popular with dads who wanted to pass on their love of magic tricks to their children.

Lexi told me—on good authority as her aunt had been in the shop in the week it opened—about another room at the back of the shop. I wandered through the shop, past the kits of magic tricks, promising to teach anyone magic into a room with a sign above the door. *The Apothecary* was lined with shelves containing jars of herbs, little boxes with crystals, and other items I didn't know the name of. Handwritten labels on the items listed ailments and cures and uses in casting spells. There were books on herbs, crystals, and magic, Lexi's aunt said the owners moved here after visiting Spirit Town during our annual festival. The lady, dressed in a flowing black dress, looked vaguely familiar. I couldn't shake the feeling I'd seen the lady recently, but younger. Could she have been one of the teens in my travels with Grandma?

Lexi would know her name. I'd been lucky to have chosen Lexi to work on the paper with me. She was kind and friendly with everyone, she had an eye for detail, we worked well together, and through her family, she knew a lot about everyone in town.

Spirit Town was settled originally as a farming area. Explorers accidentally discovered its unique arable farming land. Nestled between the mountains and the river, whatever was planted, flourished. The earliest record of a settlement here included a family who distilled the purest, finest whisky ever tasted in this newfound land. It was known as the town that brewed the best spirits - hence the name Spirit Town. Convicts, especially those from the old country who were specially gifted in some way, found their way inland to our village. Those who shunned the social norms and chose to live life large and spirited found a haven here, in the town where everything grew.

"You don't need a magic wand to create magic here." I spun around, not recognising the voice behind me.

The footpath behind me was empty. I blinked, and yawned, popping my ears. I must have imagined it, I believed in all sorts of magic, and knew my parents and grandma were always close by, but this felt different. I walked a little faster than normal, wanting some distance between myself and the magic shop. The street was quieter now, less traffic.

The warmth of the café drew me. Comfortable, safe, with people sitting and chatting. I plonked myself in one of the booths near the front door.

"Look into your parents' accident."

That voice again. Maybe my paranormal skills were increasing, and I could pick up on beings from other worlds, realms, whatever they were called. Why though? What did they want me to know about my parents?

"This is where you are hiding!" I welcomed the sound of my oldest friend's teasing. "I have roped Lara and Jon in to joining us for a cuppa." Seamus shuffled along the seat next to me. "Have you ordered yet?"

"Not yet. I was about to message you to see if you were up for a cuppa or maybe food." I scribbled a note to myself on the mini notepad I always kept in my jacket pocket. *Check microfiche.* The microfilm at the library wasn't as comprehensive as the one at the newspaper. My parents made sure their archives catalogued the history of our town, for future generations, they said when I asked why. I never thought I'd be using their work to investigate their deaths; what I thought was a single person accident on a damaged country road. Brake failure the cause, according to Jon's predecessor.

"Earth to Beth ...What do you want me to order for you?" Seamus' voice dragged me back to the present, to the warmth and safety of the café. Lara and Jon arrived at the same time. Back in the present, amongst friends. I'd returned to town to mourn, not thinking for a moment that I'd stay. Now I couldn't imagine living anywhere else. The voices, whether a message from beyond the grave, or a result of a lack of sleep, were strange, but there was probably a reasonable explanation.

"Strong coffee and a piece of Evie's salted caramel cheesecake." My mouth watered, craving the tangy yet sweet, melt-in-the-mouth delight that was on the special board.

"Has there ever been a person with unique gifts on the Spirit Town police force?" Jon asked, as Seamus and Lara returned from placing our order.

"That might make life as a policeman in this town easier, or a whole lot more difficult," I mused over the intricacies of having a gifted member of the force.

"There were rumours, when I was little, of some police who used unusual methods of policing. I guess it's like any job, having the ability of second sight would come in handy, but being extra strong, or x-ray vision might get you into trouble." Seamus chuckled. "As long as the person was using their gifts for good and not for evil, as they say."

"I remember different stories too. I think some people with special powers would feel drawn to careers where they would help others, so being a policeman makes sense. The same as being a doctor or a teacher. It wouldn't always be easy. If they were unfairly accused of something, it would be tricky to prove their innocence." I'd been friends with one of the children of a policeman who had to leave town, even though he hadn't done anything wrong. "My friend's Dad saw crimes, before they were committed. Some of the townsfolk were a little disgruntled at being arrested, before they actually committed the crime."

The table fell silent.

"It's a tricky balance," Lara said, voicing what we were all thinking.

Seamus spoke softly. "In the last month or so, since the Spirit Festival and the incidents that preceded it, the residents of Spirit Town have embraced their gifts in a way I haven't seen in years. We're seeing an influx of people using their powers. Little things like doors opening before the person reaches it, which is handy if you are carrying something heavy or have your hands full. I've seen groceries following people to the car, rather than being carried, which I still find weird to watch. We used to be cautious about using our powers in public." Seamus pointed to the saltshaker in the middle of the table. It slowly moved towards his knife.

Lara gasped.

"I didn't know you could do that." I was genuinely surprised. We hadn't played with, or even talked about, our gifts since we were eighteen.

He shrugged. "I don't mess around, normally. Seeing what was going on in town, I became curious as to what I can do."

"Since the festival, I've seen a lot of new people coming into the shop. They're interested in learning about being healthy. Some are curious about supplements to enhance magic." Lara's fingers were idly spinning her fork around while she spoke. I could tell she was trying to puzzle something out. "I don't think they're all gifted, but I assume some of them must be."

"I'm curious as to how we can run a census to see how many people with gifts currently live on our town. I mean I don't want to know who they are or where they live. I'm intrigued about numbers of residents who have powers, versus those who are 'normal', and the types of gifts they have. Analytically, not gossipy. I know that sounds weird," I admitted.

Before Seamus or the others could comment about my census idea, Evie arrived, tray in hand. "So sorry this took a while. I'd no idea we'd be so busy this afternoon." Evie delivered a plate of salted caramel cheesecake and a cup of steaming hot chocolate to each of us. "Seamus did ask if I could bring a plate of wedges and sour cream as well, so I have, although I don't know if they go well with dessert." She grinned as she placed a bowl in the middle of the table. It was piled high with potato wedges, with the skin on, and bowls of sour cream and sweet chilli sauce for dipping.

"Thanks Evie. It's perfect." Lara spoke for the table.

The food smelt delicious. I couldn't wait to taste the cheesecake, the right mix of sugary sweet and salty goodness. Before sinking my fork into the front of the slice, I finished my train of thought. "My census idea is for another day. Today's question is who created the power blackout, and did they mean to or was it accidental? Were the thefts last night linked to the blackout, or opportunistic?" I took the first bite of the cake, and the flavours didn't disappoint. An explosion of gooey caramel, subtle salt and the other ingredients, were as I imagined. I sipped the hot chocolate, and my taste buds did a happy dance.

"Could this be teenagers? Teenagers today have a much tougher time growing into their powers than we did," Seamus mumbled, between mouthfuls. "Maybe I'll check in with Agnes and Mike and see how they're going." Mike and Agnes were members of the gifted community who met weekly to share ideas and show others with powers that they're not alone. They helped teenagers who were discovering their powers, as it could be a difficult time, and things tended to go awry.

"Margie and I meet every week for a cuppa and a chat. Since the incidents around the festival, her children have been learning more about their gifts. They're not being bullied. I could ask her if they have any idea of who may be involved, if we think it's kids," Lara suggested. Margie and Clive and their children had been suspects in the last mystery. They were victims of a corrupt mayor and a couple of bullies.

"Would it be inappropriate to contact Mrs Marigold or Mr Moore ... er ... I mean Agnes or Mike, on a Sunday?" Jon had fallen into the habit of calling our old schoolteachers by their formal names, as Seamus and I had when we first spoke about them. I smiled to myself, it was difficult for me to stop calling Agnes Mrs Marigold despite her asking me to, earlier this year.

"I'm sure they would be as keen to help and solve this problem as we are," Seamus replied, taking out his mobile. "I've Mike's number, I'll send him a message."

It was my phone that beeped first. Lexi's message asked if I could meet her at the paper. "I'm going to catch up with Lexi, looks like she came into work after all. I'll check in later." I didn't mind missing out on the wedges, so I scooped another mouthful of cheesecake up with my fork.

"She's at work on a Sunday? It's a long weekend," Lara asked, raising her eyebrows.

"The paper is still due out on Tuesday, even with the long weekend. She has a family thing tomorrow. We had the paper ready for print, but she wanted to make sure to add something about last night's events. It won't take long. I want to go for a walk after that. As mayor. To listen to anyone who wants to talk about what happened." I stood up, taking one last gulp of my sweet drink. "I know it's Sunday afternoon. On a long weekend, people tend to stay out and about later than they normally would on a Sunday. Especially when weird things are happening." I didn't mean to sound like an authority on our town. After all, I'd only been back a relatively short time, and only become involved in community in the last few months.

"I'll text you if we have a meeting with Mike and Agnes," Seamus said.

I nodded my thanks and waved at Evie as I left the café. The main street had emptied, I laughed to myself, I was wrong about the townsfolk hanging around. The wind whipped around my legs and stung the part of my face not sheltered by my scarf. I shrugged further into my coat and walked the few metres to the newspaper office.

Lexi greeted me with a smile as I opened the door. "Before you ask, I'm not going to use your office while you are mayor. I can still see and chat to any customers and write and organise the paper from here. I can see what's going on outside, who's about to come in. Plus, I have our meeting room to spread out the copy paper to plan. The best of both, and I don't have to worry about keeping your desk tidy." She grinned.

"Thanks so much for coming in on a Sunday," I said automatically, my mind a little distracted by the ominous voice earlier.

"Seriously, Boss?" she said with a huge smile. "I enjoy putting the paper together and doing the research. I love the challenge and accountability, and it's great to have on my resume." Lexi tapped on the keyboard; her fingers faster than mine would ever be. "It's not forever. The balance of the term you have until the general election is about two years, isn't it? Whether you choose to run again or not, well that's up to you."

"Hmm. You're right as usual. Honestly Lexi, I love the buzz of being the mayor. I'm keen to get some initiatives in place for the community. I think after the two years I will be ready to hand over to someone else. I do miss being here, writing the articles, working with you. I'm lucky you're so good at this. Now, what did you want me to read?"

"I LOVE THE WAY YOU have told the facts, and not speculated at all about the cause of the power failure. The question at the end, inviting anyone with any information of the break-ins and the thefts to contact the police station; it'll be interesting to see if anyone does." I handed Lexi her laptop back after reading her article.

"Oh good, because I was wondering if I should be raising the point that there are gifted people in our community who may know more about what happened. I don't want to cause any issues." Lexi frowned.

"I know what you mean. I was thinking along the same lines. People here are already considering who the culprit could be. We don't need to add weight to those thoughts. What do you think about a series in the paper, not linked to this incident in any way; about some of the gifts our community have? We could have the talented artist one week, the person who can manipulate the weather the next. That sounds lame as I say it, but I want the point to be that we as community have many gifted amongst us, not just supernatural." My voice trailed off as I tried to work out the best way to describe what I was trying to convey.

"Yes! Let me think on it and when we meet on Thursday, we can nut out the details. Did the paper run a similar campaign, many years ago? I think I saw something when I was looking through the microfiche." Lexi made notes on her mobile, tapping quickly with her thumbs in the way people younger than me could.

I rapped the table with my fingernails.

"What's wrong?" Lexi could read my code for something was on my mind.

"You mentioned microfiche. I wouldn't normally ask, but on Tuesday could you please look up a traffic accident a couple of years ago. A double fatality." I had trouble getting the words out. My tongue was sticking to the roof of my mouth, and it had nothing to do with the salted caramel.

Lexi looked at me with a frown. Her eyes widened as she realised why I was asking.

I shook my head. "Please don't say anything now, we can talk about it another time. If you don't want to look it up, I understand. I will explain why, next week sometime."

She nodded. "Of course I'll research anything for you, no explanations required. Where's my cute little friend? I thought you might bring him for a visit."

I smiled appreciatively as she changed the subject. "I was out when you messaged. I'm trialling him at home by himself. Speaking of which he's been there a while, I should head back. Unless you want me to look at anything else?"

"Nope, that was it. Do you want a lift? It looks cold out there. That way I could have a cuddle." Lexi's face lit up. She loved Spark almost as much as I did.

"Oh, go on then. I'd love a lift home." As she locked up, I sent a text to Seamus, so he knew I was okay to get home.

The message back answered the question I had about when we were meeting the gifted community.

Meeting with Agnes tomorrow.

Chapter 3

Being mayor means I don't get any free time. Weekends are quiet, but with regular options to meet towns people socially. Invitations to events, such as birthdays, a trivia night, and special box seats at sporting events were occasions for getting to know residents I mightn't otherwise have met. A long weekend was a welcome mini break.

"Today is just for you, me, and Buddy," I told my little familiar as he wound himself around my ankles. My whole body tingled at his purring, his energy, and the bond between us. With Spark in one hand, and a carrot and an apple in the other, I opened the back door. A blast of cool air met us. "Maybe it's inside for you and me, after we feed Buddy. A book, a cup of peppermint tea, a quiet start to the morning." My jaw relaxed at the thought of the peace and quiet.

Buddy met us at the foot of the stairs. He happily munched on the carrot while Spark explored the verandah. "No matter how often you come out here, you always find something new, don't you? And you, Buddy, it's lucky you don't feel the cold. I'll come back out and visit later, but for now it's time for us to go back inside."

Mum's garden looked pretty, even during the winter months, with roses, geraniums, and gardenias growing alongside the natives. The herb and vegetable garden lay dormant for the most part during the winter. I was glad most of the garden looked after itself, and that dad's fences kept Buddy away from the garden. My parents had made deliberate choices that minimised the amount of mowing and maintenance in the backyard. When the weather warmed again, I'd find the time to get stuck into the garden and make sure it remained the way Mum and Dad intended. So much time, effort, sweat, and hard work had been expended creating it. Grandma taught me the basics when I was little. It was my parents who spent the hours in here, after Grandma passed, making a peaceful, beautiful space for Buddy, the birds, and any other creatures that visited. Every time I walked outside to see Buddy I was taken back in my mind to when they were still alive, and Grandma too.

A muffled *thud* pulled me out of my reverie. It came from inside the house, or maybe the front verandah. Spark bounded ahead of me, fearless as always.

Nothing appeared to be disturbed in the kitchen or the hallway. I opened the front door, not expecting to see anything unusual. At the top of the three steps that led from the path to my little verandah sat a wooden box. Around thirty centimetres square, and half that high. Looking along the path I couldn't see anyone.

"I wonder what we have here?"

Spark nosed the box, put his left paw on it, then walked back inside. "It's not dangerous and you'd like to look at it inside? Okay then little fella. Let's find out what this is all about." I picked up the box, which was lighter than it looked and took it inside.

The wooden box, made from balsa wood, but old balsa wood, reminded me of one of the old cigar boxes where Dad used to keep his collection of old quill ink pens. It must have been stained at some time throughout its life as the wood was darker in patches. There was writing, now faded, on the side; I couldn't make out the words. I did notice the tiny pin nails at the corners and along the sides; this was likely handmade; rather than a repurpose of an old box, although whoever left it on my front step may have repurposed it from its original use.

Unlike traditional cigar boxes, the lid came away as a separate piece. On top of a pile of sepia photographs, was an envelope addressed to me.

Curious, I opened the envelope, taking out the folded piece of old parchment paper, gently opening it so as not to rip it along the creases. The font was a flowery handwritten cursive that could've been written yesterday or hundreds of years ago. Fine black pen lines, the sense I got from holding the paper was that the author knew exactly what they were doing and that it was important.

Beth,

There are secrets in this town, deep, dark secrets, hidden for years. Only a few are left who know this truth and it is time to pass the information on to you.
You are the keeper of words, the truth seeker.
It will be uncomfortable and challenging, but it is time for the unveiling.

As I read the words again, I still had no idea what the writer intended to convey. I decided to let my intuition take over. As I picked up the first few photographs, I recognised some of the local landmarks around Spirit Town. Photos of the floats and celebrations during previous years Spirit Festivals, people dressed as all kinds of magical beings, depending on the year's theme. Were these photos in the archives at the paper? I could ask Lexi to investigate, she'd love that assignment. I flipped one of the photographs over, hoping to find a description written on the back. No words; a series of numbers —a date—on the back. That was something at least. As I took out the next few photos, there seemed to be an order to the way they were packed in the box: landmarks, then the festival, now local shops and businesses.

Before going any further, I cleared away the books and papers I had laying around the table in the formal dining room, now used as my messy pile of *I'll get around to it one day.* The ornate old tea chest in the corner held some of Grandma's favourite pieces of material. Whenever I opened the box, the smells and memories of her came flooding back. I chose a cream-coloured piece of calico and laid it flat over the dining table.

I positioned the photographs in piles from left to right, in the order I found them in the box. The back of some of the photos of the businesses did have names as well as dates, faded and barely legible, and spanned back at least one hundred years, the earliest date appeared to be *1891.*

Was the next pile of photographs families? Farming families? Original inhabitants and their descendants? I recognised some of the faces, but I was guessing at this stage. Underneath the pictures were some papers, old, worn, and creased. At the top of each piece of paper was written a year. Underneath the date, each page contained a series of incidents, or events. Under *1991* the list included:

Car running off the road.
Unseasonable snowstorm in September
Local farmers dams turning to pineapple juice.

A list of incidents—the results of experiments carried out by the gifted in our community. I'd seen a book with these items listed before, a long time ago. Seamus's family were the unofficial record keepers of the unusual incidents that occurred in town. In an unwritten understanding, the police kept their records in a way that didn't arouse suspicion with their hierarchy.

Spark stood up on his hind legs, his paws tapping my knees. I lay the pieces of paper on the table and picked up my kitten. My back muscle twinged as I moved. How long was I sitting looking at the papers? I'd left my mobile in the kitchen and had no idea of the time. I jumped as I heard footsteps on the front verandah. Seamus opened the front door before I could get there.

"Are you ignoring your phone? What if someone needed our local mayor?" My old friend said with a smile, handing me a takeaway cup.

"Do they? Need the mayor?" I asked, sniffing the cup. "Yum, mocha, thanks!"

"No idea. I was bored. The farm seems to run itself these days, I've organised myself out of things to do, since becoming a council member. I have people in the shops, working on the property..." Seamus reached out to pat Spark, who purred loudly in appreciation. "I tried to think of a hobby, apart from food, but that just made me hungry. Evie's was open, and as you weren't answering, I brought the mocha to you. What book are you reading that you ignored me again?" Seamus referred to my tendency on a Sunday to ignore my mobile if there was a book I was particularly engrossed in. As I placed Spark back on the floor so I could drink my mocha without him chasing it, I wondered if he had known Seamus was there, when he climbed my leg. Of course he did.

"Much more interesting than a book. I was on my way to my phone to ask you to come and see what you made of this?" I pointed to the piles of photographs and papers strewn across the dining room table. "I found all of this in that box on my front step earlier this morning. There appears to be some sort of order to the way it was placed in the box. I was looking through these papers, which are similar to the information kept by your family." I stopped talking and let Seamus rifle through what I found. I stood back, sipping my mocha. Spark danced in little circles around Seamus' legs, then with a look at me, he raced off to his water bowl, lapped up some liquid and came back and sat on my feet. Spark loved Seamus as much as I did. Friends since the first day at kindergarten, and apart from the period when I moved to the city, best friends always.

"Would the paper have similar records and photographic history of the town?" Seamus asked after a few minutes. "The lists under each year do seem the same as our family book, but I'd have to double check. Jon's still reading through the volumes I gave him, to get a better understanding of how police cope with the idiosyncrasies of our town. The station seems as safe a place as any to leave the family records."

"I'm going to get Lexi to conduct some investigation of our records, the microfiche, and the other files we have archived. What do you make of the letter that's addressed to me?"

"Of that, I've absolutely no idea. Did your parents, or maybe your grandmother, keep any records over the years?"

"Maybe. It never interested me, growing up. Since I've been back, I haven't looked around or gone through cupboards. I threw myself into my work." I'd been putting off going through Mum and Dad's things, and Grandma's room too.

"There comes a time when things need a little bit of a re-fresh," he said gently. "I can help if you like."

"Thanks." I sighed. "But not today." The idea of going through their things was exhausting.

"What if we chose one spot and focused on it?" Seamus looked around the dining room. "This room for example? There's not too much in here, compared to say your grandma's room, which from memory was as cluttered as a library inside a witch's apothecary. It's been twenty years since I ventured in there. As nice as she was, her room always scared me. I thought you were so brave when we used to sneak in there to gawk at all her trinkets."

"I'd forgotten about that! I loved her collection of herbs and hand drawn illustrations. You loved the rocks she kept in the glass case. Do you know I haven't been in there since I came back to town. Will you help me have a look through here?" I pointed around the dining room. "Then we could go into Grandma's room and see if the rocks and herbs are still there. I mean, that letter is clear that there is some information I need to know. If you're here, it won't be so bad."

"I guess I could spend some time helping out," Seamus said. "As long as we can grab some food later, sleuthing will be exhausting work."

Luckily, our formal dining room was the least cluttered room in the house. I'd commandeered the table as a desk. I opened the left-hand side door of the mahogany sideboard. Two sets of six cork placemats with matching coasters sat on the top shelf. The lower shelf contained a couple of long, lace table runners. "Nothing exciting here," I commented, not sure if I was disappointed or not.

"This side is the same, a few tablecloths, three vases, and two cork mats for serving hot food," Seamus agreed from the other side of the furniture.

On the matching mahogany side table was a white marble container, which was empty, I checked; a tall side lamp with a big tannish coloured lamp shade, and a photograph of me as a child of about eight, with Grandma, Dad, and Mum. A couple of wet, hot tears spilled from the pool welled up on my bottom eye lid. I brushed them away.

"Is this one of your grandma's chests?" Seamus knelt in front of the only other piece of furniture in the room. I joined him in front of it and ran my hand over the elephants carved on the lid. I slowly opened the chest; the lid lay back against the wall. Unable to speak, I gently lifted out bundles of calico, lace, and assorted other pieces of material. I placed them reverently on the polished wooden floor. Every cell in my body vibrated with energy, connecting with memories of time spent with Grandma so long ago. Rather than sadness, the electricity was uplifting and energising.

"What's this?" Seamus lifted out a long, flat cardboard box that we found other the piles of fabric. He carefully opened the lid, to reveal Grandma's collection of photographs.

"I haven't looked through these since Grandma passed, well maybe once, with Mum. Grandma had photographs of our family going back several generations, including before they immigrated from Scotland." I passed some of the photographs to Seamus, glancing through another handful, not sure what emotions I was feeling.

Spark poked his head out of the chest. I'd been so engrossed in looking through the photos I hadn't noticed my kitten hop into it. "Hey, Spark." I gently lifted him out, placing the material back into the chest, and closing the lid. "We can leave Grandma's photos on the dining room table." I stood up, my knees creaking as I stretched.

"I know you might not believe this, and I can't believe I'm going to ask, but can we start in Grandma's room, before we eat?" Seamus asked. I noticed his energy immediately, like a ten-year-old kid allowed to play with his favourite toys.

"You won't be scared, in Grandma's room?" I teased.

"Not with you by my side to protect me and fight off any ghosts," he joked back.

"You won't fade away, not eating food for a while?" It was like old times, like we were kids again. We both felt it.

I didn't know why I kept the doors to Grandma's room and my parents' room shut. I told myself it was to save heating and cooling, but it was more about memories. I focused on work and when I was home, I didn't venture into either room. Until now.

I turned the old brass doorknob slowly. "You'd think there'd be a musty smell considering it's been closed for months, since before Christmas." Instead, the familiar smell of rosemary and lavender that I associated with Grandma wafted out to greet us.

"I'll open the curtain and the window anyway," Seamus said. Let some light in so we can see what we are doing."

The four-poster bed with the rainbow square blanket drew my eyes straight away. Grandma knitted each of the squares for the quilt. She taught me how to knit and we sat one winter, when I was ten, making enough squares for this blanket. It used to lie on my bed.

"When I returned home, I moved it back into Grandma's room. There were too many memories to try to sleep under this every night."

"I thought it was your blanket," Seamus said, touching the edge of it. "You loved that you and Grandma made it together."

The shelves along the wall were the same as I remembered.

"Have these jars been here since Grandma passed?" I heard the awe in his voice.

"I think so. Although Mum probably came in here. I didn't pay that much attention, I'm sorry to say. I wish I'd taken more notice when they were trying to teach me." I counted twelve jars of herbs, all labelled in Grandma's handwriting. Her books were tucked in on the shelf below.

"This is the box of rocks." Seamus gently touched the wooden box next to the books. "Only they're crystals, aren't they?" He shook his head with a smile on his face as he read the labels on each little box. "Amethyst, rose quartz, citrine, turquoise, jade, jasper, hematite."

I opened the top drawer of the dresser under the shelves. "Come and have a look at this," I whispered. Under five silk scarves, all various hues of her favourite purples and greens, was an old-fashioned ledger book. On the front, written in black pen were the words *Town Records 1960 – 1975*.

As I flipped the pages over, Grandma's handwriting described incidents including some freak weather events, unusual time slips, taking some residents into the past by twenty years, other residents flying through town on broomsticks, during a school play of Macbeth, and rose bushes with chocolate flowers.

"This is like my family's ledger. I didn't know your family kept records too." Seamus said.

"Neither did I. This is the only one in this drawer, so maybe the others are here somewhere too." I opened the remaining two drawers, which contained some blouses, nightshirts, and leggings, but no other ledgers.

"Aha! There're more books in here." As he opened the cupboard under the other set of shelves, to the left of the dresser, he moved his hand with a flourish. Spark pounced at his hand to see what all the fuss was about.

I turned around to survey the rest of the room. The sewer's dummy still wore the white lace dress, although the fabric was a little yellow around the edges. The floppy straw hat on top was adorned with silk roses. Grandma's gardening hat. On her bedside table was an old porcelain doll that used to sit on her bed, and her glasses. Something was missing but I couldn't put my finger on it.

"The last date I can find on the ledgers is 1991," Seamus called from his position cross-legged on the floor, where Spark was chasing his hands.

"The year she passed away," I murmured. "The question is, did Mum continue keeping track of everything?" I stopped, tears filling my eyes. "They must've been sad that I didn't ask about any of this or keep up the family traditions." Instead of sitting in a blubbering mess on the floor, I opened the wardrobe doors. In front of me hung a row of dresses and cardigans, all familiar, as if she were in the room with us.

I looked at my feet as Spark decided it was the perfect time to start tickling my toes.

Seamus gently closed the wardrobe drawers. "Enough investigating for one day. Sleuthing always makes me hungry. How about we go for a drive and find something to eat?"

I knew what he was doing, and I loved him for it. My best friend wasn't an empath in the same way I was. He didn't pick up on the moods and emotions of everyone else all the time. He shared that connection only with a few. I was one of the lucky ones. Since that first day at Kindergarten, Seamus has always been able to read me. Sometimes it was frustrating, other times annoying. Today I was pleased. "Yes, I should feed you." I grinned. "Seriously, I'm grateful you spent the day sneaking around our house, like old times, helping me solve the mystery, or maybe finding new mysteries to solve."

"I was hoping for burgers and fries at the café," Seamus said, following me to the kitchen. "Although I'm sure whatever you cook will be fine." He feigned fear at the thought of my previous culinary accomplishments.

I poured some water into Spark's bowl, and a handful of kibble into another one. I kissed the top of his head as I put him on the other side of the gate, that I drew across the kitchen doorway. "Just for a little while, my friend," I whispered to him. "I don't want you to get into the papers or the photos in the mess I've left in the dining room." He waved his paw, an indication he understood my words, and walked over to his cushion. We left to the sound of his purring as he kneaded it into the right shape for a nap.

Chapter 4

"I thought the café would be busier, it's one of the only places open today," I commented as we walked into the café, where there were only a handful of people at the tables.

"I think there's a pumpkin throwing competition at Apple Tree. A lot of people are off camping for the long weekend, or on their way back, getting ready for work and school tomorrow." Seamus kept an ear out for all the goings on around our village. Apple Tree and Flowerville, the two villages closest to Spirit Town, had interesting names, but as far as I knew, their residents were more normal than the inhabitants of Spirit Town.

"Beth, Seamus, what can I get for you?" As usual Evie was full of smiles. She'd a way of making everyone feel like we were long lost friends coming to visit.

"Do you have any specials left? I was looking forward to your burgers and fries, but the slave driver here kept me busy working all morning." Dramatically placing his hand to his forehead, Seamus pretended he was exhausted.

"I don't believe it for a minute," Evie countered. "I'll bring your meals over soon."

"Can we have some water too please, Evie?" I asked, suddenly thirsty. "Some pineapple juice too, if we may."

We chose the booth that could be called our regular. When the corporation from the city threatened our town's annual festival we'd met here almost daily, to share information, ideas, and solve the mystery. Since becoming mayor there'd been less opportunities for catching up at the café with Seamus, Lara and Jon. Each time I entered the café its 1960's style décor made me smile. I knew the older residents loved the checkered tablecloths, the jukebox, and slide in booths, while the more modern features were a hit with the younger locals. The bench with charger points was always popular, and kids loved the play area.

The pineapple juice sent waves of energy around my body. I must've been dehydrated. I tried to remember when I'd last drunk some water. In all the excitement of the last few days and finding that box on the verandah, the last time I picked up my drink bottle must've been early this morning. Before my morning coffee. The juice worked its magic.

"Were we meant to be meeting Agnes and Mike sometime today?" I asked.

"Oh yeah. I forgot in all the excitement of mysterious boxes and photographs. Mike and Agnes will meet us this afternoon around 4 o'clock at their regular meeting place." He looked at his mobile to confirm the time. "Lucky, we remembered, it's after 3pm already."

The old church had been decommissioned years ago. The gifted community made the necessary repairs and met weekly to share their skills and talk about any specific issues. I'd only recently made peace with being a member of that community. Swallowing my pride and admitting my mistakes resulted in their community endorsing me for mayor. Without their blessing I wouldn't have seriously considered taking on the position.

"Are we meeting the others there?" Referring to Lara and Jon, my question was answered a few seconds later when I heard the bell signalling visitors to the café. Lara and Jon slid into the seats next to us.

"Is this an early dinner?" Jon asked, eyeing the burgers on front of us.

"Late lunch," Seamus answered with a mouthful of chips. "The mayor kept me busy this morning. I dragged her away from the project or I would've faded away to nothing,"

"That's never going to happen," Lara said good naturedly. "Any project that keeps you away from food must have been intriguing."

I let Seamus finish eating. He was clearly in need of sustenance after such an exhausting morning. "Someone left a box on my front step. It contains photographs and information – a history of some of the interesting events and incidents that have occurred in our town over the last hundred years. We compared it to some of my family photographs and records, like the records Seamus's family keep. I didn't even know my family kept records."

"Why would someone leave the information on your step? Especially if your family already keep the information themselves?" Jon asked.

"That's a good question. There was a note to me, suggesting that I needed to uncover some secrets about this town. Well hidden, uncomfortable truths." I paused, taking a bite of my burger. I didn't know what to think about the implication that my parents may have been keeping secrets. Not that I would've paid attention, when I should have, but it didn't sit well with me.

"Do you think this is linked to the power outage and the break ins?" Lara asked.

"The was my sense of it," I replied. "I think I'm going to have to compare the information in the box with the records my family have, and maybe even the early editions of the local paper. I think Lexi would love that job." I thought about the best way to manage this mammoth task as I took another bite of the burger. Evie's burgers were homemade with love, and deliciousness. Did fairies have secret ingredients they shared that made these even better than normal burgers? I suspect they did.

"Look! I can see the cogs turning, as she works out what tasks she is going to delegate to each of us. Duck, run or hide before you get assigned homework," Seamus joked.

"You're not far off," I admitted. "I was wondering what records Agnes would have and if we should compare with them." I rolled my eyes. "So much for a peaceful long weekend."

"I think we talk to Agnes and Mike about it and see what they say," Jon agreed. "After we ask about the blackout and the thefts. Sorry, Beth, but that's got to be the priority at the moment. Unless you feel threatened in any way. I don't want us caught going down a rabbit warren if the answer is more straightforward."

I looked at Jon over the last of my burger. "Thanks, but I don't feel like I need any protection.

"Admittedly it appears nothing is straightforward in this village," he added with a wry smile. "I'm glad Fred works at the station here full time now. I get the feeling June is going to be a busy month. My boss has confirmed we can get more bodies if we need to."

The others were thinking along the lines as I, worried about the latest strange events. It appeared I could read their thoughts. I decided to keep that quiet, until I figured out if I could control it. I didn't want to be always tuning into what they were thinking.

"Time to meet the others." Lara glanced at her phone. "Are we all going in one car?"

"Why not? That's the perfect excuse to come back here for an early dinner." Seamus grinned. How he could be hungry after that meal—well, that was one of life's mysteries.

THE TINGLING OF GOOSEBUMPS along my arm happened every time I got close to the place where the gifted community met. For twenty years, I blamed the community in general for an event that happened when I was a teenager. I'd since made peace with myself and the leaders of the community, having initially mistaken their work—which was to support the gifted in our town—as something more sinister. Once I understood their motivation was to teach and guide others, I wasn't so scared of their powers, or mine.

The old building that used to be a church looked neat and tidy enough from the outside but dilapidated enough to discourage tourists from hanging around outside or trying to get inside. Part spell, mostly the hard work of the previous generation of people with extraordinary abilities. It was a safe haven where those with abilities could meet, discuss concerns and fears, and learn how to use their gifts safely.

"Welcome." Agnes, my old teacher Mrs Marigold, met us at the door. Her long, grey hair was piled up high on her head, she didn't look any older than when I sat in her classroom. Her signature outfit, black and purple skirt and a black jumper, a long silver necklace which held a key, a tiny bottle and a piece of amethyst, felt comfortable, now that I no longer feared her.

We followed her into the room, where on a Thursday people with magical abilities were provided a safe space to learn and practise. This afternoon there were nine chairs arranged in a circle near the front of the space. Additional chairs were stacked up near collapsible tables and one with an urn and some paper cups along the left side wall. The wooden floorboards were well worn from years of meetings and before that, church goers traipsing mud and dirt and leaves in and out of the place that provided safety and shelter. The bare wooden ceiling where a fan and a light hung, precariously low to the heads of the taller amongst the group. Neither were used much. There wasn't much call for a fan in the cool Spirit Town weather. In summer, the open doors and windows allowed in a breeze. The electrical system had been re-wired, with recessed lights providing adequate lighting. I wasn't entirely sure that the teachers themselves didn't illuminate the area without the use of modern conveniences.

"I would like to introduce you to Trudie and Boris." Agnes indicated the couple sitting in front of us. Trudie's dark hair was tied back into a severe ponytail, and glasses perched on her beaked nose. Boris was balding, with tufts of fluffy brown hair above his ears. "They are here from the High Council. Although there is no record of all the people with powers in any one area, the amount of supernatural energy is monitored. Apparently, we have been emitting an unusually large amount of energy recently, and so they decided to pay us a visit. They've been tracking the opening and closing of time slips opening into Spirit Town for years, since before you were born. The portals don't happen often, but when they occur, they need to be monitored. We must be careful not to change the past."

Mike walked in behind us. Tall, skinny and maybe ten years older than us, he wore shorts, even though it was single figures outside. A thick khaki coat and worker boots completed his outfit. "Sorry I'm late." He shook hands with Jon and Seamus, and nodded to Lara and I. "Boris, Trudie, nice to see you again."

Jon spoke up, taking advantage of a gap in the conversation. "I'm particularly interested in the electrical blackout and the thefts at the chemist and the newsagent. Do you think someone from this community may have been involved? Was it an accident, due to experimentation with magic, or was it a deliberate act?"

I watched Agnes, Boris and Trudie. Nothing in their facial expressions gave away what they were thinking, the aura around the strangers was guarded. I knew I wouldn't be able to see their thoughts. I couldn't bring myself to interrogate Agnes' thoughts, if I could help it. She used to be my teacher; she gifted me with my familiar. All sorts of respect and boundaries that I wasn't going to cross.

Agnes nodded, with a wry smile. I gave her one in return. She read my thoughts.

"It's not the kids," Mike said, referring to the group of teenagers experiencing their powers for the first time. "They're coping well with their newfound abilities. The extra training we are providing has eased most of the erratic behaviour we were experiencing. The tension amongst the teens appears to have eased. There are still cases of broomsticks falling from the sky and fairy floss and caramel dropping from the older trees in the park. On Saturday there were reports of whiskey pouring from the waterfall a few kilometres out of town. We've shown each of the teens how to repair their mistakes."

"Do you have any ideas about the blackout? Would the thefts be opportunistic, rather than planned to occur during the loss in electricity?" Seamus asked Mike.

It was Boris who answered. I shivered; his deep voice was ominous, not evil, but scary. "We've been tracking an anomaly; there appears to be a tear in the time continuum. People are popping in and out of times past. From what we can tell, one of these time slips resulted in the blackout." Mike and Agnes exchanged a glance. I couldn't tell the intent, but there was hidden meaning behind it.

Trudie continued, her voice as firm as her colleagues. "The thefts were unusual. Supplements and stationery were taken. Like someone was stocking up for some reason. We're looking into it. Our investigation won't impinge on yours." Her cold, blue eyes skewered Jon.

"So, if Jon and his team do their due diligence and you do yours, if we find anything we collaborate?" I turned on my bossy mayor voice as best I could. I didn't like Trudie or Boris. We didn't need outsiders telling us how to manage things. As far as I could tell, Agnes, Mike and the others seemed to have everything under control. I felt oddly protective of our gifted community.

"That sounds fair," Mike spoke first, turning to the others, who nodded. Boris started to speak, until Trudie landed a swift kick to his shin.

"I have another somewhat unrelated question if I may." I turned towards Agnes.

"Whatever you say here is safe and stays within these walls," my old teacher responded.

"I'm interested in how we have traditionally tracked what happens in our community. Is there someone who is charged to keep secrets, keep tally or account? When the river turns to raspberry cordial, or the broomsticks fly overhead? When crimes are committed by a member of the gifted community? I know Seamus' family have always done so. Are there others?"

"I sense you're asking for a reason. Are you happy to share that reason? I understand that you haven't always been so interested in this side of our town, or your personal family history?" Mrs Marigold asked, not unkindly.

I realised I trusted Agnes, and while I didn't know if I trusted the others, intuition told me to go ahead and speak my mind. "I received a package on my front step this morning. A note in a box containing photographs and a history of our town's magical side, suggested there was a truth I needed to uncover. Seamus and I found some more photos and information in my grandmother's room. It made me wish I'd paid more attention as a teenager and an adult. I'm paying attention now. I'm ready to learn and help our community, our town. Not as mayor, as me, my ancestry." I stopped as a wave of exhaustion swept over me. I shifted in my seat.

"That's a discussion you and I can have another time," she said gently. Not normally a word I would have used for Agnes, until that day when she left Spark with me. Even then, I was still a little scared.

I sensed that was all I was going to get for now. My eyes told her I understood, we could discuss this later. If there was something to discuss about my family, I would prefer it be out of hearing of Boris and Trudie.

Agnes turned to Mike. "Noting the information Boris and Trudie shared, I think we could talk a little more about the training program."

Mike nodded to Agnes and addressed the group, "I won't name anyone, but the group of teens we're working with, have discovered a time slip. They're most likely the cause of it but haven't yet mastered how it occurs. One of the others can see the past, as if it happened to them, instead of their ancestors. We have discovered, accidentally, that one of the group can slip in and out of the past in their sleep."

"Are they able to change the past?" Lara asked quietly. "Are we likely to wake up one day to find a different village, or that some of our friends don't exist anymore?"

Boris frowned at Agnes and Mike. My toes wriggled uncomfortably, relieved the disapproving look wasn't aimed at me. I'd shrivel into nothingness if the glare had been levelled at something I'd said. I squeezed Lara's hand as Boris responded, "Unlike what we watch on the idiot box, it takes a powerful magic to change the past. We can't bumble around and suddenly we are our own parent. That takes intent, going back deliberately, which if I understand correctly, isn't the case here."

"The teens would be happy never to visit the past again. They are fascinated, and terrified at the same time," Mike assured everyone.

"How do you propose we tackle the issue?" Jon asked scratching his shaved head. It must be cold, during winter to keep his head almost bald. His police jacket did look like it would keep him warm, but it needed a hood. "We seem to have several challenges. Let's tackle the most pressing problem first."

Mike nodded. "I think it'd be best if we continue to work with the youth. They trust us, we can help them resolve their current challenges. The power outage may have been accidental, but I'd bet my reputation that the thefts weren't. The break ins don't feel like teens playing around."

"Trudie and I will provide you with a solution that will stop them opening time slips. We can ensure if any of the teens decide to use intent to open one, that it won't be as easy for them next time." The heat of Boris's eyes, staring at us, wasn't evil as I had first thought. He wasn't trying to intimidate us. I felt his need to do the right thing, made him appear abrupt. I loosened my shoulders, the knots in my stomach unclenched, as I realised Boris and Trudie weren't threats after all.

"Have you tried a locator spell, for the items that were stolen?" Trudie spoke up.

This time it was Agnes who frowned. "We don't encourage use of our gifts in that way," she said sternly. "We stay right away from police investigations."

Jon wiped his forehead with his hand. I felt his exhaustion. "I don't know how I feel about using magic to solve crimes. It would be quicker, but ultimately, I can see issues with that. Like an invasion of privacy, or too many people trying to do the work of the police. I'd prefer to stick to old fashioned police work, if no one minds."

Lara asked timidly, "What if we think it's someone stockpiling items to cast a spell or cause trouble? Would using magic to find the culprit useful in that instance?"

"Maybe. It's still feels like prying, invading people's thoughts," Jon mused. "There could be merit in using supernatural sleuthing powers occasionally. Let's first interview the couple of suspects Fred has identified may have committed the thefts. There's intel that a gang from the city moved up here and are responsible for break ins in the surrounding towns. If that doesn't pan out, I would be open to learning new ways."

Agnes nodded to Trudie and Boris. "If you show Mike how to close the time slips with the teens, I can show Jon the locator spell if he needs it. Is there anything else you need from us?" I wasn't reading Agnes, but I knew that she didn't like these people and was glad of the opportunity to send them back to where they came from.

Trudie answered, her fingers weaving a picture, like knitting a scarf, the image floated from her lap, over to Mike. To me it looked like feathery light, with sharp colours. Was it a code of some kind?

Mike folded the image, once it landed in his lap, tucking it in the pocket of his coat, like you would a piece of paper. It was fascinating, seeing a spell shared like this.

A flash caught my eye, and I looked to see what Trudie was doing now. Her chair was empty. So was the chair where Boris sat, seconds before.

"I'm sure they'll be back in a flash if they see anything else that worries them. We don't see them for years at a time, then out of the blue, *bam*, they're here trying to blame us for random occurrences." The sarcasm in Agnes voice was impossible to miss. In a much calmer voice, she turned to Lara and asked, "Will you have some time this week to assist me with an inventory? The new magic shop has an apothecary section stocking many of the herbs we use regularly, which is great. I'd like to work with you to make some of our products more readily available to our regular folk, who might be a little too hesitant to visit the new shop. They feel more comfortable walking into a health food store." Earlier in the year my intuition told me Agnes and Lara may be related, though I wasn't aware of Lara possessing any powers. Maybe this collaboration had been what I sensed. My newest friend was attractive in an understated way, demure, and she always dressed beautifully. I sensed she'd no awareness of the lightness of her aura. People were drawn to her healing light.

"I'd be honoured to," Lara said. "Would you like to call into the store tomorrow and we can coordinate something?"

As Agnes was speaking an image played in front of my eyes, like a scene from a play. She turned to me, her eyes connecting with mine, from behind her thick framed glasses. "Beth, do you want to share what you saw?"

"I don't exactly know, so I'll describe what I saw," I admitted, not too surprised that Agnes picked up on my second sight. "It was in the past, because Grandma was there, and my parents. People gathered in a large room, not the church. There was a lot of noise, yelling, someone called for calm and quiet. Maybe a town meeting, in an auditorium, like at the school or a community hall. It would have to be thirty years ago, more if my grandmother was there? The timeframe may be wrong." I hesitated. "Describing this out loud doesn't make sense. My second sight may be picking up on the images in the photos we were looking at this morning."

"It could be," Agnes agreed. "I suspect it's a message, but you'll need more time, quiet time with your familiar, to work out what the message is conveying."

"That makes sense. Since the time slips opened, I've been drawn to times past. I find myself in my dreams wandering through Spirit Town years ago. I don't see my parents, but I have seen Grandma, and other faces that are familiar. I'm there to learn about my ancestors and uncover a mystery. Whatever is happening now, is linked to events of the past. I feel like I'm seeing only small parts of the puzzle pieces." I wondered silently what Trudie and Boris would have made of that. I glanced at their chairs, half expecting them to pop back at any moment.

"I'm guessing the newspaper office would have records of all meetings in the town, dating back as far as its first publication. More details than the council records, and more accurate than depending on anyone's memory," Mike suggested, as he stood and stretched. Dressed in a long-sleeved shirt, and shorts, as he had every day during my high school years, I wondered whether his magic accounted for the fact that he didn't feel the cold. No that I knew what skill he possessed.

"I'm going to ask Lexi to do some research back through the archives. She loves that sort of stuff nearly as much as she loves video interviews," I said, referring to the video interviews we had conducted with some of our older residents earlier this year. We asked them for their memories of Spirit Town's past festivals, and we aired their stories on the local radio and television stations. Lexi loved technology, talking to people, and listening to their stories. Loved uncovering the history behind events.

"As mayor, you have the added burden of knowing about our gifted residents. You have that balance in you, able to tread evenly amongst both. Seamus, you have it too." Agnes' piercing green eyes softened. "I see you both making a difference while you're on council." Agnes still gave off a teacher vibe. A strange but welcome friendship seemed to be developing between us.

I noticed my friend squirming in his seat, as uncomfortable as I was with the praise.

"Okay, so we all know what our next steps are." I tried to take the focus off our skills and back to the current issue. "Jon, do you need any more information or assistance?"

Jon fiddled with his notepad. "It sounds like Mike, you, have the time slips, and the cause of the blackout under control, so there's no need for me or Fred to spend time on that. We'll investigate the thefts and can keep you in the loop. Which I think is the key. Honest and open communication with this. Between us."

"I'll come into the station after work tomorrow," Mike told Jon. "I'll let you know how I go with the teens and closing the time slips."

"THANKS FOR DROPPING me home." I unsuccessfully tried to hide a yawn with my hand.

"I guess you aren't inviting me in for a late-night snack." Seamus smiled mischievously.

"We just left the café." This time I didn't try to hide my yawn. "It's been a long, exhausting weekend. If you don't mind, I'm going straight to bed. I'll see you tomorrow."

I waved as his ute left the driveway.

Spark was pleased to see me. He snuggled into the crook of my arm. "I didn't mean to leave you here so long by yourself. Let's go see Buddy."

I held out a carrot. Buddy's warm nose nuzzled my hand. Spark batted Buddy gently with his paws. The sheep didn't mind. He munched until the carrot was gone. His teeth made short work of the apple, too.

"I should be exhausted, Spark, yet now that I am back with you, my energy is buzzing. It's bedtime, but a cup of chamomile tea for relaxing my energy first." I poured a little milk in his bowl. Spark enhanced my dreams and my abilities. I'd no idea how I could be exhausted and so full of energy at the same time.

Chapter 5

Spark woke me, dragging me from my dream before I had a chance to solve a riddle. Holding Grandma's hand, we were about to step through a mirror into the past, when my familiar patted me on my right cheek with his paw, insistently.

Before I could ask what was wrong, I heard a noise. In the house. I whispered to Spark to stay on the bed and grabbed the cricket bat that sat beside the door to my room, and tip toed out towards the sound.

Bang.

The sound the kitchen door made banging shut, when I forgot to hold the old wooden door for it to close behind me. Bravely I tiptoed to have a look. There was no one in the kitchen, or anywhere in the house. The dining room door was open, but the photographs and papers appeared untouched. I wish I'd paid more attention to the way I'd placed everything on the table, or that I'd put them away when I got home. Hindsight isn't helpful to anyone, though.

With the torch that sits near the kettle in case of a power outage in one hand, I opened the back door to check on Buddy. He was near the back step, which wasn't odd, he must have thought I was on my way out with food. I nearly tripped on my gumboots, which normally sit to the right side of the back door, not sprawled over in front of the door. A possum could have done that, but it was more likely that the intruder knocked them over on the way out. I shone the torch out over the garden. I wasn't about to try to navigate the series of gates Dad built to keep Buddy away from the vegetables and the cottage garden. It was too dark for that. How the unwelcome guest faired I wasn't sure, but I couldn't see any movement or disturbance amongst the plants.

I patted Buddy on the nose. "Time for more sleep Buddy. It's not time for carrots yet." I sat the gumboots back in their allotted space and as I closed the back door I bolted it. Seeing as I was wide awake and with no idea of the time, I turned on the kitchen light and started the kettle boiling. While it hissed and heated the water, I decided I should check for intruders, theft, or damage.

The old pantry, now an adorable library, beckoned me. I loved sitting in there, reading; partly because I loved books and partly because of fond memories of sitting on Grandma's knee as a small child, while she read stories to me. The light bulb reflected in the little mirror, placed to make the room feel bigger. I squinted as the light hit me straight in the eyes. Once I regained my sight, satisfied nothing was disturbed in my reading room, I turned off the light and closed the door.

I listened in the quiet as I poured myself a cup of peppermint tea. No noise interrupted the silence in the wake of the kettle whistle. I walked past the dining room and opened my bedroom door, letting Spark join me. He followed me into Grandma's room. It looked the same as earlier in the day. "There's no indication that the intruder ventured in here," I told Spark, who was exploring the room. He followed me as I checked inside the wardrobe.

I decided to check the wardrobe in my own room, although I would have been surprised if Spark let anyone get in there. It was empty, apart from my assorted clothes, shoes, and winter woollies.

Looking at Spark for reassurance, I put my cup on the table in the short hallway and picked up my familiar. I held him tight as I opened the door to my parents' bedroom. "I haven't been in here since the day of their funeral," I whispered. "I guess it's time to chase away the ghosts, the melancholy, and get on with things."

The door made a creaking sound, as if it was groaning at being disturbed after so long, standing guard in the one position. I reached my free hand for the light switch. I flicked the switch, but the room remained in darkness. "The light bulb must have blown," I whispered in a shaky voice. Spark nudged his nose against my chin, comforting me, giving me the strength to walk into the room. "I'm not telling Seamus I was too scared to walk in here in the dark," I said with a little more conviction. Spark placed his left paw on my arm. I was grateful for the added vote of confidence.

I'd walked the steps to their bed so many times in the dark as a child. After a bad dream or I felt sick, I'd tiptoe from my room to theirs. Ten steps as a ten-year-old to the closest part of the bed from the door. On the bedside table there should be a lamp. My leg bumped into the bed after I counted four steps. "Of course, my legs are longer now," I told Spark, as I tried not to rub my knee. I fumbled about in the dark, no light shone in from the blanket thick block out curtains. There was a sliver of light from my room, but it was at the wrong angle to provide any clear light for my quest.

Thud!

I knocked something off the bedside table. Spark didn't jump in my arms, so I figured I was safe – determined to scare away the ghosts now. Gently moving my hand around the table, I couldn't find a lamp at all. I'd been away from home for a long time, of course they could have changed things around, redecorated. "Mum used to have a flashlight in the drawer." I told Spark. "I wonder if it's still there." Thankfully, the ornate metal drawer handle hadn't changed, and the drawer opened easily. My fingers connected with what felt like the round handle of a torch. I grasped the metal handle and pulled the item from the drawer. I pressed the button. An eerie yellow glow emitted from the torch. I aimed it at the floor; confirming it was a book I knocked off the table. I placed it gently back on the table. The yellow light revealed a reading light on the bedside. I pressed the button, turning it on. Not much had changed in the room. The bed quilt was a rich tapestry of greens and ambers. Mum begun the quilt, a long time ago. Grandma had patiently shown her how to hand sew the tiny stitches. I remembered the day Mum put the quilt in the cupboard, promising Grandma she would finish it one day. I smiled. She'd finished it. Grandma would have been smiling from heaven, watching as her daughter sat sewing the pieces together.

All the drawers in the dresser were closed, as were the wardrobe doors. Nothing appeared disturbed. I put Spark on the floor, letting him explore. I lay back diagonally on the bed, looking up at the ceiling. I'd forgotten that the ceiling in this room included an embossed pattern around the light fitting and in the corners. Circles and curves, I used to lie here and count them until I fell asleep, if I snuck into my parents' bed in the night. My gaze drifted to the mirror above the dresser.

My brain registered there was something odd about the mirror, but I couldn't put my finger on what. Suddenly so tired, my eyes followed the line of the glass. Not a crack or a chip that I could see. I must be imagining things, so I rolled onto my other side. Spark was playfully batting a ball of fluff. Still, intuition drew me back to the mirror. I climbed out of bed. My fingers ran gently around the edge of the mirror, and behind it, looking for a hidden message. Nothing. I tilted the mirror up a little to check underneath. No hidden pieces of paper. I glanced at the glass and gasped. I'd somehow angled the mirror, so it caught the pattern around the ceiling. The names Lyle, Madge, Beryl and Beth appeared, embossed in the cornice of the ceiling, as clear as if the words had been there all along.

No matter how I moved the mirror, I couldn't make out any other words. With my mobile phone I snapped photographs of the whole patterned strip. Maybe I could hold it up to the mirror in the bathroom, in the morning, when the lighting was brighter. I was curious, and tired, and whatever messages the mirror would reveal could wait a few more hours.

I yawned. "No damage, nothing stolen. I must've left that door unlocked. The wind caught it, flinging it open and slamming it shut." My voice echoed oddly in the silence of the night.

Spark gave me a look that said neither of us were believing those words. I scooped him up, turned off the light and left the door to the room slightly ajar.

On an impulse, I opened Grandma's door too.

My half-finished peppermint tea wasn't warm anymore. I drained the cup, checked the front and back door were locked, turned off the light, and carried Spark back to bed.

Chapter 6

I tossed and turned until I couldn't lie still any longer. The images, faces, and words being yelled or whispered at me when I closed my eyes were disturbing. My stomach was cramping, I wasn't sure if I wanted to throw up or if the nausea was all in my head—a reaction to a lack of sleep and an overactive imagination. Spark was curled up right next to me, I tried to keep still, tricking my body back to sleep.

The minutes on the clock ticked over so slowly. When at last I decided to get out of bed, the time read 4:27am.

"Come on Spark, let's start the day." Spark opened his eyes and looked at me as if I were crazy. I knew his sleep was as disturbed as mine. "You can always stay there if you want to," I added, knowing that he would choose to be wherever I was. As my feet touched the floor, I was grateful for the trouble my parents went to, to keep the house warm during winter. The automatic timer on the air conditioning unit set the heat to come on at four in the morning. Still, I slipped my feet into my fluffy boot like slippers.

The messages and whisperings from my dream, if that's what it was, were still lingering, and slightly disturbing. Faces unfamiliar to me, and voices distorted by the dark. The words were too muffled for me to make sense of. Messages, warnings, threats, or a weird dream? I couldn't make sense of any of it.

"Shower first, Spark, if you want to stay there longer."

A detour to the kitchen, so I could turn on the light and the kettle on my way to the bathroom. In the shower I tried alternate bursts of hot and cold water, making a point of shaking my fingers to release any remaining pent up negative energy. I wriggled my toes for good measure. I tied my long, dark brown hair up on top of my head into a messy looking bun. If I got it too wet, it took ages to dry. I didn't bother with a hairdryer; I was rarely patient enough to make it look styled and elegant.

The inspection of my wardrobe in the early hours revealed my old baggy purple tracksuit. Having forgotten I'd stashed it at the back when I'd returned to town, I chose to wear it this morning. It wasn't for going out in public, but it was warm and cosy. I would change into work clothes later. I slipped on my comfy boot slippers, well worn, the wool on the inside warmed my toes.

My kitten was prancing around the kitchen like he owned the place. It was so cute! Opening a tin of his food, I placed his bowl on the floor next to his water bowl. "Coffee for me this morning," I told Spark.

It was dark and cold by the time on my laptop read 4:53am. Too early to be going out to feed Buddy, I snuggled into my fluffy boots and my tracksuit.

The beginnings of an idea that I couldn't quite catch, niggled in the back of my mind. Was it a hangover from the disturbing dream that I hadn't managed to wash down the drain this morning, or something else? "Maybe I'm feeling out of sorts because I've been going through Grandma's things and in Mum and Dad's bedroom," I told Spark as he came over to snuggle on top of my left slipper. He gazed at me, licking his paw daintily with his tiny pink tongue.

As I picked up my phone, I remembered the photos I'd taken in the early hours. I headed to the bathroom. The mirror reveal wasn't as earth shattering as I imagined. When I held my phone up to the mirror, apart from the names of my family that I'd read previously, the other images were just that, images.

Back at the kitchen table, I discarded my mobile and scrolled through the emails on my laptop. Nothing urgent in my personal drive that needed my immediate attention. I wandered into the dining room and flipped through the papers on the table. If I sat here for too long, I'd be late for work. "Being a Tuesday after a long weekend, I should go into work early. I can focus on this when I come home," I told Spark, picking him up for a snuggle. He'd only been in my life a couple of months, but it felt like forever. "Mrs Marigold, err, Agnes, was right when she told us we were meant to be together," I whispered.

While Spark played with the tassels on my tracksuit, I opened the calendar on my laptop. The long weekend meant a short working week, which meant more tasks jammed into a shorter space of time. "Lexi can manage the paper," I told my familiar. "The shops are fine, although I'll visit tomorrow, to make sure they are going okay." I updated the calendar to fit in a visit to the paper this morning and a visit to Wynyard Street Wednesday. *Remember cake for Seamus* I jotted next to tomorrow's date.

There was a meeting with Jon scheduled, to discuss the strange occurrences in town from an official point of view. We knew the time slips and the blackout were related; I still wanted the police update on record. "A de-brief afterwards at the café with the others if we can fit it in," I added to my list for the day. It surprised me that I missed the daily contact with my new friends. It was only after catching up with them again over the long weekend, did I realise how much. I saw Seamus most days at work, though not often socially, since joining the local council we both found the workdays long and tiring.

The first sliver of sunlight glistened in from the window above the kitchen sink.

"Time to feed Buddy before I get ready for work. Come on, friend." I scooped Spark up with one hand, and with an apple and a carrot in the other I opened the back door. The gumboots stood where I left them last night. I'd convinced myself I was hearing things and that no one would be prowling around the house. "Letting my imagination run away with me," I told Buddy, as I patted the top of his head while he munched on the carrot. I squinted in the direction of the back fence, the morning sun getting my eyes at the right angle to be annoying. It must be a trick of the light, there was no way that fence post was crooked. Dad spent ages measuring, getting the fences and gates exact, so that Buddy and his predecessor, Dudley, could munch on grass, and our vegetables and herbs could grow in a garden away from our fostered animals. "I should make time to tidy up those plants along the fence," I murmured to my animal friends. "Maybe next weekend, if the weather holds." Wintertime in Spirit Town was often wet and windy and cold. If our residents were playing around with their abilities, the weather often exploded in unpredictable ways.

Buddy was happy in the house block, where it was a little more sheltered. I poured some warm water from the kettle into his water bowl, to warm it a little and stop it freezing over.

I watched Spark for a few more minutes as he wound himself around Buddy's legs, Buddy nuzzled as close to him as he could, bonding as they did daily. Most days I took Spark into my other office, to spend the day with Lexi, more for her benefit than my kitten's. Knowing he would be safe at home by himself was a positive, if there ever came a time when Lexi wasn't able to look after him at the office. We'd set up bowls, foods, a basket, and toys for him at both offices as well as here at home. "It's much easier to carry you out the door, rather than all your stuff as well," I crooned as we walked back inside, locking the back door behind me. I took him with me as I double checked all the doors and windows were locked, and all the lights in the bedrooms were turned off. "Remind me to replace the bulb in Mum and Dad's room," I sat my kitten on the floor while I changed for work.

My black and amber pants suit hung in the cupboard, my treat when I won the role of mayor earlier this year. I slipped a thicker white shirt on under it, and some thick, black socks under my black dress boots. Tying my hair back into a ponytail completed my transition from Beth to Mayor Beth. My little friend was already waiting at his carrier, while I packed my laptop into my bag.

It was a little after 7am in the morning as I locked the front door behind us.

"YOU'RE HERE BRIGHT and early." Lexi greeted me with a smile as she took the kitten carrier from me.

"I couldn't sleep, I've sorted my calendar already and I knew you'd be here, ready to work on the rest of the week's layout. My first meeting is at nine, so I'm all yours until eight thirty." I sat at the spare seat next to Lexi in the meeting room, where the drafts were spread out across the table.

"It's all under control. We have the results of the *dress up your pet in football colours* competition, including photos of all the pooches and other animals; there was even a macaw, and a python dressed in their owner's fav footy colours. Plenty of photos of the fireworks, and I added a story about the black out. Because it's still a mystery, I've written it as an ordinary glitch, that the electricity company is looking into. I wanted to make sure that's okay with you."

"Actually, that's perfect. We can downplay it, so that it's not a big mystery after all. Jon thinks he knows what happened, and it likely won't happen again. It doesn't look like the break and enters are related either." I wasn't keeping the information from Lexi, but there was no need to spread the information about the youths who were experimenting with their powers. I knew too well how scary that could be.

I giggled with Lexi as Spark pounced on Lexi's colourful shoelaces. "In addition to the microfiche task I asked about the other day, I've some more sleuthing for you, if you're up for it." Lexi nodded; eyes wide open with excitement. "A box of photographs arrived on my doorstep, and with it a list of events that occurred in town throughout the last sixty years or so." I handed her a photocopy of the list." When you have time would you like to compare it to our records and let me know what you find?"

"I'd love to!" Lexi clapped her hands together. "What specifically am I looking for?"

"I'm not sure, maybe anything that's different, or the same. There's something I'm meant to figure out, I'm not sure what. If I wasn't mayor, I could spend more time on it myself. You can keep that copy, the original is at home."

"I'm happy to help, I love these types of tasks. If you're thinking of anymore video interviews, I'd love that too." Her tone changed suddenly. "There is one thing though." Lexi pulled out an envelope from under her pile of papers. "This was left at the door of the office sometime after Sunday afternoon. I found it this morning. I've taken a quick look at our microfiche records and the information isn't the same." Her brow furrowed. "I may have started that conversation without the important piece of information. The documents in this envelope refer to incidents relating to your family. How your parents died, and your grandma as well." Tears filled her eyes. I experienced the familiar sting as salty water welled in mine.

She handed me the envelope. "Our records show your parents died in a car accident at the railway crossing when a truck lost control, pushing their car onto the track in front of a train track maintenance cart." Her voice broke. I leant over and embraced her, partly to comfort her and partly because I wasn't sure what I was feeling or what I should say. I nodded that I was okay for her to continue. "Our records show your grandmother died after a short illness." She stopped. Neither of us knew what to say next. Spark chose that exact moment to climb up onto Lexi's lap and swat her curly hair that was hanging on her left shoulder, before leaping onto my lap.

He broke the tension in the room. We laughed at his antics.

I knew he meant it was my turn. I kissed him and placed him back on Lexi's lap and took a deep breath. "Grandma died of a mystery illness. I thought it was a heart attack. I blocked out the information at the time. It was too painful. I always meant to ask Mum for the details, but I never got around to it. When I lost Mum and Dad at the same time, I tried to block that as well. I worked as much as I could. I shut the door to their rooms and never stepped foot in them again. Until yesterday."

Lexi nodded; a couple of tears trickled down her cheek. "I'd do the same. I wish I could suggest how to validate what's in this envelope. I know the police records here lack detail, but doesn't Seamus's family keep records as well?"

"Yes, they do. Weirdly, yesterday I discovered that my family were also keeping records." I took a deep breath, calming my energy. I sensed the spirits of my parents and my grandma in the room with us—their energy keeping mine under control and tranquil.

Lexi looked at me with concern. Spark looked over, his eyes searching mine, for signs of distress. Our bond grew stronger every day. Assured he didn't have to worry about me, he jumped from Lexi's lap and headed into the kitchen. I heard his tongue lapping up the milk I knew Lexi would have poured out when she arrived.

"The box of information I received on the weekend suggests that there is more to their deaths than I know." I held up the envelope. "I don't know what's in here yet, but I think it's pointing to a criminal or evil element in Spirit Town." I shuddered, involuntarily, as if a shadow passed over my shoulders. "That sounds melodramatic when I say it out loud." I laughed it off.

Lexi smiled, although I could tell she was being brave. "We solved the mystery of Max, the trouble making mayor. I'm sure we'll figure this out too." She glanced at her laptop. "It's 8am. I know you want to get ready for your day. I have the paper under control. Do you need me to do anything else?" She held her fingers over the keyboard, ready to make notes on her electronic calendar.

"You're the best Lexi!" I said as I stood up. "I'll be okay for now. I may ask you to assist me with the research and piecing together the information once I have a chance to work it all out. This is something we'll need to work on together. Not because I'm mayor, but because you can be objective about the information we find." I gave Lexi a hug, her long black curls tickling my nose.

I briskly walked the few hundred metres from the newspaper office to the council chambers. The early June morning hadn't yet thawed on this side of the street, the sun was still steadily climbing above the buildings. I shivered again, wondering if it was the cold or a sinister undercurrent that seemed to be seeping into my bones.

Stop being so melodramatic. You are the mayor! Focus on practical mayoral stuff. The rest can wait until later, I told myself.

Early morning was busy in Spirit Town. People on their way to work, taking their children to school. I smiled *good morning* to everyone I passed in the short distance from one building to the other. I watched as George, our council gardener, drove his ride on lawn mower into the local park area. The sun crept into half of the park, melting the frost and dew enough for an initial drive through to keep the grass pristine. George, a friend of Dad's, used to teach at the high school.

Growing up, I never considered myself part of the local community of residents with supernatural abilities. As a teenager I both loved and feared the idea of my powers, conflicted about the balance between magic and logic. As soon as I finished high school, I left to attend university, to follow my dream of becoming a journalist. The excuse I told myself, that I didn't want to be a part of the magic group in our community, wasn't true. I'd been scared and acted rashly, choosing to run and hide, to be 'normal.' Recently I'd made peace with my emotions about what happened years ago. I was ready to embrace my 'magic' abilities.

A flash of colour outside the glass doors at the front the council chambers caught my attention.

"Deep in thought as ever." The familiar and welcome voice of my oldest friend distracted me. I was glad for the interruption to my thoughts.

"I'm planning my day, and I have a favour to ask." I turned to Seamus as we turned the corner to the back entrance of the council chambers.

"Official or unofficial?" he countered mischievously.

"Both. First things first though. My 9am meeting is with the development committee, talking about some long-term plans in the local farming area. Then we have our ten thirty with Jon." Seamus nodded as I continued, "Do you have time to see if Lara and Jon would be free for an early lunch straight after, to debrief? The meeting with Agnes went well, but I want the chance to have a chat about it all." We met at the café afterwards, but we'd all been too tired to discuss any of it in detail.

"Make time for lunch? Of course!" He grinned. "I'll book us a table too. See you on the flip side." He held open the door after I unlocked it. As Seamus walked along the corridor to his office on the left, I turned right and opened the door to mine. Everything was as I left it on Friday afternoon. The hairs on my arms prickled; a clear indication that something needed my attention. On a more detailed look around the room, nothing appeared out of place. I wiggled the top drawer of my filing cabinet. It was locked, as it should be. I touched the key on the lanyard that I kept tied inside my handbag. The key was there, the other copy Seamus stowed somewhere safe for me. The other three drawers of the white metal cabinet were locked. I lifted the blind at the window behind my desk. The window latch secure, as I expected it to be. As I sat at my deep red mahogany desk, I noticed the drawers on the left-hand side were slightly open. Did I leave my desk drawers unlocked on Friday? I couldn't be sure.

The contents of the top drawer hadn't changed; a few black, red, and blue biro pens, a thin black marker pen, a stapler and a single hole punch. The twenty-centimetre clear plastic ruler, with a few rubber bands twisted around it, and a couple of pencils, and an eraser. The contents of my pencil case from home. The previous occupant of the role emptied the entire contents of the office when he absconded with a bucketload of money, all of which was returned when he was arrested for fraud. The police weren't able to recover any of the items he'd stolen from this office.

The second drawer held a couple of notepads, a physical diary, and a couple of lined notebooks I used for taking notes at meetings. A box of pens in case I ran out of my others. I'd hit the ground running, with enough time to make sure I what I needed for the role.

The larger bottom drawer should have been empty. Where I stowed my bag when I was in the office. All the mayoral papers were stowed securely in the locked filing cabinet. As I opened it, a large brown envelope sprang up, as if it'd been hastily shoved in the drawer. I pulled it out, comparing it to Lexi's. Turning both over, no distinguishing writing or markings evident. Intrigued, but aware of the time, I reluctantly tucked both envelopes into my bag, and my bag into the bottom drawer.

I chose not to have a secretary but kept my office door open so clients and councillors could find me when they needed to. When I met with clients and the door was closed, the table outside the door contained a book and pen for people to tell me they called by, why, and how I could contact them.

The prickling sensation that began on the hair of my arms, washed in waves across my body. Some trace of magic intent on the envelopes or their contents calling me. Doing my best to ignore the buzz emanating from the envelopes, I placed my notebook, and a blue pen, to the left of my laptop. I'd make time after lunch to look at the envelopes. Seamus wasn't joining me for the meeting with the planning and development team. That didn't faze me, though I appreciated his input when we discussed long term plans for the area. His knowledge of farming and agricultural practices as extensive as his ability to make others feel at ease.

Greg, Drew, Kim, Jamie, and I fitted comfortably around the table in my office. The councillors each made a point of making a cup of tea from my stash on the bench when they could have easily brought their own from their office. I noted the power play, because it was unusual. I'd only been in the office for a few weeks, but I didn't normally get the feeling I was in the way, as I did today.

"It is important that we get this right," Greg said, tapping his pen on the table as he spoke. I'd have understood the implication, that I was new and not up to the job, without my newfound ability to read thoughts.

I bit my tongue, wanting to ask what the project was, but decided to wait, to give the others a chance to brief me properly. From the information I'd been able to gleam, this initiative wasn't new, and while the previous mayor supported it, considering his actions, the team decided it appropriate to get my sign off to progress the project.

"You might not have heard about this project; there are plans to redevelop the old whisky distillery, the one on Riley's Road." Greg was tall and built like a star footballer. He may have thought by standing up to deliver his speech it would intimate me. It didn't.

"Are we, as council, supposed to develop small businesses? Surely, we should be considering applications from residents," I countered.

Drew, a thinner build to Greg, but of a similar age, covered his mouth as he coughed, stifling a laugh.

Kim was a little older than me. I'd seen her at the Thursday gatherings at the church, although I wasn't sure what her skill was. She tentatively held up her hand.

I nodded at her. "You don't need to put up your hand to speak," I added gently.

Kim spoke from where she sat. "The distillery is being proposed by the Wilson family. Their ancestors ran one of the most popular bespoke distilleries locally. Their plans include renovating the old buildings on their land and building a new restaurant and conference area. Ideally, they'd love to teach some of the skills that were passed through the family. I'm sure Greg meant to say this is one of the developments in front of us to approve, and that we all recommend going ahead."

Greg gave her a look I couldn't decipher and sat heavily with a *harrumph*.

Drew slid a manilla folder across the table to me. "It's all in there. We've agreed to the development proposal. We conducted a site visit a month or so ago. The Wilsons have funding from the bank. Phase one is the build and the re-build of the existing structure. We don't expect you to respond straight away. If you could review it all, and let us know, by the end of the week, if you agree with what you read, we'll go from there." He hesitated, then continued, "Of course, if you have any questions, please let any of us know. We can bring Kev or Kath Wilson in to provide more information."

"There is another proposal, I'm not sure whether Seamus has mentioned it to you." Kim slid another folder over to me. "Some of the farmers have been approached to contribute their skills and resources to an agricultural college. As with the distillery, there's a building that could be updated to code and used with minimal time and effort. They're cautiously keen, as long as the council supports it, and it's a legitimate company offering to establish the college. They don't want to get caught up like Max did."

Drew slid a thumb drive towards me. "I've put together a PowerPoint presentation. If we have time we can talk you through the key points of both applications. Before you ask, initial research indicates the training organisation is legit and nationally accredited.

I plugged the USB drive into my laptop, pressed a couple of buttons on a remote and motioned to the television screen on the shelf. I made notes as Drew, Greg and Kim took turns in speaking to the slides. Seamus hadn't mentioned it, probably because we were both cautious about being seen to be influencing each other where council business was concerned. Still, a heads up would have been good. A single ding on my phone indicated ten minutes before my next meeting.

"I appreciate you bringing these two development proposals to my attention." I caught the eye of each of the people sitting around the table as I spoke. "It is the first time I've heard of either of them. In future I'd prefer to be kept informed ahead of our meetings. When sending email invitations, please attach all documents. You'll have my response to both concepts by close of business Friday, if not earlier." I decided to trust that my team, and if I needed more information, I'd ask. "Is there any other business?"

No one spoke, so I stood up. "If there's nothing else, I've another meeting in a few minutes." The others stood, murmuring *goodbye* as they gathered their belongings and left.

I skim read the documents. I saw the benefit of a college to teach permaculture as well as traditional farming techniques. Classes in making spirits and craft beers sounded like fun too.

Chapter 7

"You're pretty chilled, considering the power went out again." Seamus walked into the office, as I gathered my thoughts. I considered the last meeting successful, despite the way Greg behaved at the start. I was very different from Max, and it'd take a while for the councillors to trust me.

"Oh ha, very funny," I responded.

"Try turning on the light, or better still, let's make a cuppa before our meeting," he suggested.

I flicked the light switch several times, my anxiety rising as nothing happened. The same with the kettle. I jiggled the cord and the jug a few times, as if that would help the electricity work.

"I spoke to Mike." Seamus gently placed his hand on my arm. I stopped playing with the electrical cord and let my arm drop to my side. "He thinks the teens were accidentally responsible. He convinced three of them not to play around with their powers until he can teach them how to control it. The fourth one though, wanted to go back through into the past. Apparently, he likes the cars in the forties."

Suddenly my desk light and office light both flashed on. I jumped as the kettle burst into life.

"There you go! Problem solved." I could hear the relief in Seamus' voice.

"I guess it makes sense that it might take Mike a couple of attempts to convince them. When we first discovered our abilities, we wanted to try everything. It was exhilarating, powerful. As long as no one gets hurt and there's no crime wave." I frowned at the kettle, as if it the blackout was its fault.

"Any chance of a cup of tea? It's been a crazy morning," Jon asked as he and Fred entered my office. "I hope you don't mind, but I wanted Fred to brief us on the latest."

"Welcome Fred." I found a fourth cup in the cupboard under the kettle, thankful that I'd picked four of mismatched mugs from the back of the kitchen cupboard, when I set up my office. I meant to pick up matching mugs from the op shop, but I never seemed to get time. "I hope black tea is alright. Or I can grab the milk from the kitchen."

"Black is fine," Fred answered. Jon nodded his agreement.

"The power failure this morning." Fred referred to his notepad. "It only lasted nineteen minutes." He glanced nervously at Jon.

"Mike rang and confirmed that one of the teens tried to travel back through the time slip. Fred here is still coming to grips with this piece of information. Which is okay, it took me a while to understand the specific skill set of some of the residents of this village. I'm sure you don't want to hear this, but some residents have reported incidents of break ins over the weekend and this morning." Jon glanced at the tablet in his hand. "I can give you a detailed list of the incidents, but I don't think that would help."

"Another weird thing," Fred flipped through his notepad. "The break ins seem to be mischievous; I mean nothing was reported as stolen, but doors unlocked, windows opened, gates knocked open."

"Do you know if the incidents were reported by those gifted people in our community, or across the whole village?" I asked on impulse.

"I'm the wrong person to ask," Jon responded. "It's not like there's a list of residences of powered people versus 'normal', or is there?" He scratched the top of his head, a sign he was processing the conversation. "Why do you ask? Do you think it's important?"

"It's a hunch I have. I'm not sure yet. If the break ins are related to the time slip, maybe it's their ancestors knocking on their doors inviting them back to the past? Although that's weird, even for here. I don't know much about time slips, but I'm adding it to my list of things to research." I looked at Seamus, who nodded. I took that to mean he'd investigate the anomaly.

"From a mayoral perspective I'll need to reassure the residents that we have everything under control, although I'm not aware of any concerns. Do we know that the outage wasn't a 'normal' outage because of a storm somewhere, a truck running into a power pole, or something?" I asked. "I know the teens have admitted to causing it through the time slips, but I'm keen for as much validation as possible to share with the community."

"There are no reports of any accidents," confirmed Jon.

"Over the last three months, have you seen any patterns of criminal behaviour that we should be concerned about?" I asked him. "I mean, considering that those in the gifted community can sometimes accidentally cause mishaps. Apart from the newsagents and the chemist, have there been other thefts locally?"

Jon scrolled through the tablet before responding, "I would have to say since Max was jailed and the Castle Home was built in our neighbouring town, we've seen a reduction in suspicious activity. There've been a few freak storms and other issues, the results of the younger generation practicing their skills, but Mike has their training under control, except for the time slips."

"It's only been a couple of months. Are you looking for any specific pattern?" Seamus asked.

"I'm not sure, I want to keep on top of everything." I flicked through my notes of the prior meeting. "The meeting with the planning and development committee went well. There are a couple of applications, one for a distillery and one for an agricultural college." I avoided looking at Seamus, knowing his face would give away whether he'd known about both projects. "The proposals included renovation of some buildings and possible upgrades to local roads around the region in the next few months. There's some spare money to make sure the roads in the area are repaired ahead of the tourist season. Apple Tree and Flowerville are going to beautify their main street, inspired by feedback on the aesthetics in Spirit Town with the cobblestones, the new lighting, the paint scheme, and the garden beds. Both towns have applications for new businesses, taking advantage of the increase in tourists with the Castle Home development in Flowerville. That will be an interesting, as we know, their complexes often squeezed out local businesses." I paused. "Seamus, do you have anything to report? I know you met with some of our local farmers who were talking about innovations in farming practices."

"They're keen to implement some more permaculture principles which will work in well with the college. I can suggest some farms that would be open to work experience for the students. They want to diversify in other ways too. The other towns have farmers growing citrus and stone fruits and all kinds of edible flowers and plants for essential oils. Our farmers are keen to work with the others and see if we can add another tourist attraction – an edible farm trail in the spring and maybe autumn as well. Also, sunflowers, and mushrooms."

"Would it be useful to have a town meeting, to talk to the residents, assure them that there is no threat with the black outs and the break ins?" Fred asked, bringing the meeting back to the key issue at hand.

"Thanks for getting us back on track." I smiled at Fred.

Seamus fiddled with his pen. It was unusual for him to be worried or nervous. Being a councillor was a job he took seriously. He looked across the desk "That's a good idea, but not yet, until we know without any doubt that Mike has the youth training and time slips under control. The last thing we want to do is tell the community it is a supernatural thing and have it get out of hand. Our teens are self-conscious enough, without well-meaning locals singling them out."

Jon scrolled through his tablet, before closing it and looking up. "I received an email. Those individuals we thought were good for the robberies, it turns out they were in custody elsewhere at the time. They're more mainstream crooks—stealing money, jewellery that sort of thing." He looked around the table. "Should we consider using supernatural ways to find the culprits?"

"I could use my intuition to try to locate the items," I mused. "I've never tried anything like that before."

"I suggest we wait and see what Mike comes up with," Seamus suggested. "Let's at least wait another day before we decide."

I looked around the table. The others nodded. I glanced at my watch as my stomach rumbled. If I was hungry, Seamus must be starving!

"Jon, can you and Fred work with Mike and ask him to keep you updated with the time slip issue? I think he will anyway, but it doesn't hurt to ask. Ask him if he knows if the break ins could be linked to the time slips. Seamus, maybe you could coordinate the meeting in the first instance. I know you and Mike have been working closely together." I scribbled some notes on my notepad, to keep track of what I was delegating.

"I'll set up a meeting for this afternoon. Does that suit you?" Seamus asked Fred.

Fred looked at his notepad and held up his hands in the thumbs up sign.

"I think the town meeting idea has merit. Let's keep it in mind, if we need to, once we have all the information," I suggested. I stood up and stretched. The others stood up and headed for the door.

"Don't forget lunch," Seamus reminded me and Jon. "Fred, you're welcome too. I'll ring Mike on the way and let you know when we're meeting him."

"Thanks but I'll head back to the station. Happy to meet up whenever Mike is available."

"I'll bring you some food after lunch," Jon said, patting Fred on the back.

"I'll join you soon, I want to check my emails." I sat back behind my desk as the others headed out the office door. "Don't wait for me, if I get caught up here," I added, hoping that there were no red flags to attend to. I was starving.

"We won't." Seamus grinned. "But I might bring you back some food, if you don't turn up."

"I'll be there. But thanks, because I'm hungry." My half an apple at 5.30am this morning seemed a long time ago.

Before I could open my emails, I heard the external door swing open. The whoosh it made when the office was quiet, echoed in the silence.

"Excuse me, Beth, do you have a few minutes?" I recognised Mrs Marigold's voice, and I stood up and strode over to meet her at the door.

"Agnes! I always have time for you," I greeted my old teacher affectionately. I hadn't always viewed Agnes as a friend. I noted the furrow in her brow, she seemed concerned about something. "Is everything okay?" I motioned to the chair in front of my desk. I brought mine around so that I was sitting close to her.

"I hate to have to do this, but there are some things that you don't know, that you need to be aware of." Agnes hesitated and looked at her hands. Gnarled fingers, her arthritis had started long before she was my teacher. Her appearance hadn't changed much in the last twenty years. Her long, grey hair was wound up on the top of her head. A second look at her face revealed her age. I hadn't noticed her age lines before. Up close now, her energy appeared hesitant, unsure, not the vibrant, confident and strong Agnes I used to fear.

I stared at my shoes, embarrassed for Agnes, and not wanting to stare at her, to make her more uncomfortable. *I should polish my black shoes; they are looking a little scruffy.* As I pondered when I'd have time to clean my shoes, I sensed—rather than heard—a buzzing energy.

Agnes hands were weaving a story. Like watching a film on a tablet, except there was no electronic device. I watched mesmerised, as Mum and Dad sat at one side of a table, with pages of paper spread out in front of them. I observed as a line-up of people, none of whom I knew by name, each took turns at the table, talking to my parents. Each one walked away, dejected.

I frowned, a thousand questions in my head. "It looks like they are holding court and the people talking to them lost their case," I said aloud.

"You're right. I suspect you don't know a lot about your family history. I know you weren't interested in the magical side of things until recently."

I nodded at Agnes's words.

"Your Mother and Grandma were from a long line of witches who ruled the gifted community. Only ever one female born in each generation. Leaders, judge and jury. If someone practised magic with a view to harm others, they could be exiled. Your dad was a mystery. I was never entirely sure where he came from but, together with your mother, they were a formidable pair." She paused and reached her hand out to mine. I longed to keep watching, to see the image of my parents even for another minute. Instead, I held her hand in return. "Your grandmother's death, like her mother's before her, might have been the result of a malicious act. A disgruntled member of the community. There are many poisons that leave no trace after being administered."

I gently let go of Agnes hand and stood up. I looked around the sparsely decorated room before returning to my seat. I took her hand back in mine. "My parents' deaths were also deliberate. Do you know who caused their deaths, or my grandmother's?" My anger buzzed around me like an annoying fly.

"The community did suspect a few people, but we could never prove anything. We each have skills in divination and can often find the cause of mischief, but those with the darkness can block and confuse the answers we receive."

"When they died, I wasn't interested in magic and I didn't know anything about this, so I wasn't a threat. I couldn't carry on the tradition if I didn't know about it. Now that I'm mayor, are people worried that I may take the role on? Has someone been filling in the role in my absence and more importantly, are they in danger?"

It was Agnes's turn to stand up. "Mike and Jeannie have been working to counsel our youth on using their skills. Neither will agree to me or anyone else stepping into the role, we dissolved the magic council when your parents died. Most of the members were scared that if they replaced your parents, something might happen to them. We weren't willing to lose more people." She paced around my desk, weaving her hands in a pattern I vaguely recognised.

"My grandma taught me that – it's a protection spell, isn't it? I was never sure if she was a witch or teaching me to use my imagination."

"She was a most powerful witch, but she rarely used her powers. She chose instead to follow the ways of the garden witch and use plants and herbs for healing. She taught you as much as she could, hoping you'd remember it when you grew up. Others in the community learnt from her as well." Agnes stopped but I knew somehow that she was going to say, *if she hadn't been murdered you would have understood so much more.*

My mobile rang, startling both of us. I glanced at the screen, and quickly sent a text to Seamus. *Got caught up. Won't make lunch after all. Apologies to all.*

"Do you need to be somewhere? I fear I've kept you too long." Agnes moved towards the door.

"I'm right where I need to be. I've ignored this part of my life for far too long and now I need the answers. Strange things have been happening and the information you have provided is filling some of the gaps." I flipped over my notebook to the back and opened it. "Can you tell me as much as you know about who might have murdered my parents and my grandmother?"

"I'm afraid I can't. That knowledge would be dangerous and would put you in danger. I promised your grandmother I'd try my best to keep you safe. I can say that those we suspect no longer live in Spirit Town." I sensed the anger and control in Agnes, fighting for prominence. She wanted to tell me more, but she was bound by her pact to keep this knowledge away from me.

"I understand, Agnes. Please don't worry about me. It'll take some time to process this." I opened the bottom drawer, took out my bag and placed the two envelopes on the desk in between us. "These documents are similar to those that arrived at my home. One envelope was sent here, and one to the newspaper office. Different accounts of the deaths. Lexi is looking into what the official findings were and what was reported at the time. I don't know why I've been given this information. I assume there is an ulterior motive."

"Don't believe everything you read." Agnes pushed the envelopes back towards me. "I have kept you far too long. Stay safe, Beth. I'm always available if you need me."

Before I could respond to Agnes' words, she was gone.

Chapter 8

I stood up. A second later, I fell back into my seat, only to stand up again. My eyes were aching. I refused to give in and to cry. The time for mourning had passed.

"Do I pick up Spark and go home and cry? Or find out who did this? Or ignore it all and get on with being mayor?" I muttered to myself, pacing around my limited office space, wishing I was in the park, or maybe out in the bush.

"Chicken salad, mocha and a muffin?" Seamus' head peered around the door. "Even I can feel your energy, and while I read your thoughts, energy isn't normally something I pay attention to. Are you alright?" He placed the food on the table, and I let him lead me to my chair, which caused his eyebrows to arch up so much I couldn't help but smile.

"I don't want to talk about it, yet, but the short version is, Agnes confirmed my parents, and my grandmother were all murdered. They were members of a council that exiled powered people who behaved badly." I sipped my mocha, though not thirsty or hungry. I appreciated Seamus bringing me lunch, and I should eat, so I took a bite of the sandwich.

"Ah." Seamus stopped.

"You knew?"

"Suspected."

I didn't know what to say. I took another bite, savouring the crisp flavours of each of the pieces of vegetables that Evie added in the chicken salad sandwich. My favourite was the beetroot, the spinach leaves, and shredded carrots a close second. His eyes watching me, his eyes furrowed, worried as to how I'd react. I took another bite of the sandwich.

"Thanks for lunch. I mean it. You only kept me in the dark, to protect me. I promise I'm not angry." Where did my calmness come from? I'm normally way more agitated.

Seamus spoke quietly, "I was about to say the same thing." He placed his hand on mine. "Look, whatever is going on, we'll figure it out together. The mayor stuff, that's second to this."

"Thanks. It's a lot to take in. My role as mayor is tangible. It's something I can do, we can do, to give back to the community. The past's in the past. I'll figure out what I want to do about that later. The focus now is still on working out how to stop the time slips, and whether the break ins are something to be concerned about." I sipped my mocha. "Thanks again for lunch."

"What about dinner?" Seamus suggested. "I'll be hungry again in a few hours."

"Do you mind if we make it tomorrow night? I'm planning on an early night. My brain needs a rest." The familiar pounding across my temples was signalling the start of a migraine. I rubbed my forehead, as if I could wipe the pain away.

"Of course." Seamus stood up. "Your migraines are awful. I wanted to spend some time with Mike and see if I can help. Take care of yourself, Beth. We need our mayor." He walked around to give me a hug. I responded. It was good to have a friend who knew me so well.

"Back to your emails, Beth. The rest can wait."

I spent the next three hours responding to emails from locals asking how to find forms and pamphlets. I encouraged open communication, so I could hardly leave the answer to others to respond to. A couple of emails were a little more challenging. A businessman wanted to buy up local land and create a business park. I diplomatically responded that it wasn't what we were looking for in Spirit Town. A council member asking about competing priorities, and if they could pursue their business interests whilst on council. I suggested that we make a time to talk about the details.

It was after four o'clock by the time I clicked send on the last email of the day. I closed my laptop and slipped it into my bag. I added the envelopes, I wanted to read them later. After I picked up Spark.

MY FORK PUSHED THE grains of rice around the blue china plate. One of grandma's favourite plates, I chose it for my home-made fried rice; I'd been thinking about her as I made the dish she taught me when I was six. Cut whatever veggies are in the fridge; broccoli, carrot, corn, and spinach; add rice and an egg. Stir in any herbs and anything else in the fridge. We ate a version of this once a week for as long as I could remember. Not hungry, I did still enjoy the flavours, the fresh vegetables and herbs.

So many questions were swirling around in my head. There was so much I didn't know about my family, and about the town. The pounding in my head worsened. Spark patted my leg. "What's up little guy? Oh, your water bowl is empty?" I filled a glass with tap water and topped up his saucer. "Clever boy." I filled up the glass and drained the lot. "I haven't drunk nearly enough water today, thanks, Spark."

I stared at my laptop, not sure what I was hoping to find. I pulled a pile of blank paper out from the shelf under the kitchen bench. Maybe old school doodling would reveal some answers.

Have you ever wondered why Spirit Town has such a big, gifted community? Or why there doesn't seem to be the same ration of gifted people in the neighbouring towns or even in the bigger cities? Where do the gifted people go when they leave here? Where do the new people come from, those with unique gifts who join our community?

I read the words that appeared on the page in front of me. The page blank only seconds before. The scrawling script reminded me of something I'd seen years ago, when I was a little one on my grandma's knee.

Spark nudged my ankle. I picked him up and snuggled with him. "I guess I must've questioned all that once, a long time ago, before I turned away from my abilities. Now that I'm back in Spirit Town, I find myself wondering the same thing."

Are you wondering why they would come to Spirit Town of all places? They can't hide here, can they? How do they know to come here? Who is their leader?

As the words were being written I could hear the sneer in the voice. As if someone was speaking aloud. Maybe they were. A cold shiver prickled down my spine. My cardigan was too far away, and I didn't want to break this connection.

Did we, the gifted community, need a leader? The town had a mayor, which currently was me. Agnes, Mike, and the others ran the weekly meetings, helped the gifted and now the program for the younger generation. What else would a leader do?

Impatience and the irritation, in the room.

I can read your thoughts, and I am appalled that you think Agnes and her tribe are leadership material. Ha. Next you will be saying that you, and your ancestors were capable of leading and doling out judgement or punishment to those who didn't conform. I thought you were different, that you didn't care about this stuff. Being mayor is changing you!

The anger in the room was palpable. Spark's fur stood on end, as did the hairs on my arms. I straightened my back, tilting my neck so I was facing straight ahead, looking out the kitchen window at the darkness of the night. I tried to steady my voice as I spoke.

"I don't think of myself as a leader, or as powerful. I'm lucky to be in a position to make a positive difference in our town. For the gifted and non-gifted, for everyone. I've never subscribed to the us and them mentality." I took a breath and a few seconds to calm my energy. My heart was thumping in my chest. "I only learnt today about the lineage of my mother and grandmother, or that they were in any kind of leadership role. I knew them to be fair and firm, so if they pronounced a judgement, they must've had a reason to."

The back door swung open and slammed shut in one fluid, loud movement. I felt Spark jump, the same second I did. Both our hearts beating a little faster than before. The atmosphere in the room became lighter, as if a fog lifted. My ghostly visitor took his emotions with him. "Whoever that was, I've annoyed him," I stated the obvious to Spark. The action of speaking made me feel more in control.

After staring at the page for a few seconds longer, it was clear he wasn't coming back, so I stood up. As I scanned the kitchen, I couldn't see anything unusual or out of place. The time on my laptop told me it was only 7pm. It felt like the middle of the night.

"I'm not sure whether it's a good idea to go to bed now, or am I being silly?" I shook my head to clear the cobwebs away. My head felt fuzzy, a side effect of my migraine. Suddenly I was tired, bone weary. "It's been a big few days. Let's lock the doors and windows and have an early night. I'm not particularly scared." I didn't need to speak aloud for Spark to hear me. Something about the energy of my voice disrupted the silence and the heavy energy that was lingering after our uninvited guest. "I know there used to be a stash of candles in here, in case of blackouts." Spark watched as I rummaged through the linen cupboard, in the wall of the hallway. Most of the piles of linen were untouched and still folded as neatly as Mum left them. I only used my one set of sheets and a couple of towels. "I must go through this one day. Not today." The wooden box of candles was exactly where I saw it last, tucked at the side of the hand knitted throw rugs, all stacked neatly. Grandma used bright colours, blues, greens, reds, yellows and oranges in her blankets. Hers a unique mix of knitted and crocheted squares. Mum used a thinner crochet stick and thinner knitting needles. Her work was easily identified as she used more muted colours, apricot, pink, lilac, baby blue, pale green and cream. My fingers lovingly caressed each blanket briefly. I shut the linen door firmly, as if that would assist me to keep my emotions in check.

"Task at hand," I whispered firmly. "A candle in each room. Yes, I know that leaving candles to burn is not a smart thing," I told Spark. "One in the kitchen and one in my room. Not anywhere near anything that can catch alight." I made sure the candle was in the middle of the kitchen table, as extra insurance that the candle couldn't go rogue and start a fire.

In bed, I fidgeted, unable to get comfortable. I couldn't settle. What if the ghost, if that's what it was, came back and tipped over the candle and set the kitchen alight? I sighed and swung my legs back over the edge of the bed. I blew out the candle on my bedside table, and padded with bare feet to the kitchen, snuffing out the votive there. Returning to my room, I turned on the light on my beside, and the diffuser with lavender essential oil. "Not for sleep, but to ease the negative ions in the room," I told Spark, who was standing next to my right ankle, ready for wherever we were going next.

Instinct told me to check the kitchen again. My suspicions proved correct. The flame from the lit candle I'd blown out, danced in the breeze of the now open kitchen door. The one I locked tight a few minutes earlier.

By the candle flame I could see there were new words on the paper. Forcing myself to remain calm, I checked the kettle contained enough water in it for a cup of coffee. As it boiled, I re-locked the kitchen door, blew out the candle, and turned on the kitchen light.

The voice was less angry, more melancholy, I couldn't place the feeling exactly, but I wasn't scared of the ghost.

We used to be one big family. Then the women decided otherwise.

I watched new words appear right in front of me.

Your great grandmother and my great grandfather were siblings.

The inside of my mouth was dry, on fire. Desperately in need of water, mesmerised and unwilling to take my eyes from the paper, I stared at it, willing it to reveal more details. A stray blood vessel in my head pounded, noisily, like a siren going off in my head. The stories my grandmother told me; that on her side of the family, on the mother's side, only ever females born, did I misunderstand or mis-remember the stories? I wasn't very old when I heard them. I couldn't believe that my grandma would've lied to me.

Could this spirit be telling the truth? Could we be related? I concentrated as more words appeared.

Our family were always the royalty of the gifted community. In the old country, and here. Our relatives still rule over the gifted in the old country, Scotland in case you don't know what that means. Have you ever travelled to Scotland? I have. It is a whole different world over there.

It was on my list to travel to the UK and Europe. Later, in the future, when I felt in control of everything. In addition to the businesses my parents left me, as mayor, my travel plans were further away. My parents and grandmother brought me gifts when they returned from overseas. The last time they travelled, I stayed with Seamus's family for the week. The highlight of my sleepover had been helping Seamus's Dad with the farming; feeding the chickens and the horses; picking the oranges, apples, and pears; and learning to build wooden crates with left over pieces of wood. Rough pine, pallet wood. I loved the feel of the wood, and using power tools, for the first time ever. "The only time," I said out loud to Spark. I wasn't sure whether we owned any power tools. Dad liked using handheld tools, not that he spent much time tinkering in his shed. He was always busy at work or helping others in town with different projects.

Whether I voiced my thoughts or not, I was communicating with my ghostly relative and my familiar. Another gift, that of silent discussion with magical creatures, which seemed perfectly natural. As I waited for more words to appear, I realised that I didn't know many details about what my parents did. Were their trips overseas more than innocent holiday making? Did they belong to some magical royalty? "Was I that self-absorbed that I didn't notice what was happening?" I whispered to my familiar.

You were a normal teenager. They kept the truth from you.

"What truth? Who are you? Why are you telling me all this now? Did you kill my grandmother and my parents?" Spark nudged me, cautioning me to watch what I was saying. I held him close, but not too tightly. "I'm not accusing you. I want answers. The truth. If my family kept information from me, I want to know why. You say we're related. Are you real, alive, a person here and now and if so, why don't you show yourself?

My name is Jacob. I'm not the one you need to be afraid of. My family are powerful. I don't necessarily agree with them. I think it's time to work together.

I jumped, a loud noise out the front of the house startled me. Spark jumped off my lap. I followed him to the front door. The piece of carpet I placed on the polished floorboards dulled my footsteps. The sound of my blood pumping through my veins would have drowned out any steps of creaking floorboards. Would Jacob have disappeared when I returned, or was he waiting for my return? Why did he choose tonight to speak to me, and not before, days weeks or months ago?

As I unlocked the door, I grabbed the umbrella in my other hand. Not much in the way of self-protection, but better than nothing.

Immediately evident that the cause of the noise was the wrought iron table falling sideways onto the wooden verandah. "Now how did that happen?" I asked Spark as he mooched around the area. "The setting is solid, made to last. There's no wind. What would have knocked it over?" The rest of the wrought iron setting were in place. The blue pots full of geraniums hadn't moved. I peered out over the railing to the garden and the quiet street. Nothing odd or unusual.

"Let's get this table back where it belongs." I briefly considered keeping the table upturned and asking Jon to swing past in the morning and have a look. "No need to disturb him. Probably a possum or something," I murmured to Spark as I moved the chairs around to place the table back into its position at the side of the verandah.

A wave of exhaustion washed over me, as if someone turned a huge hair dryer on my back, draining me of all my energy. "Well, it is the middle of the night." I picked up Spark. "Let's try to get some sleep. Jacob, whoever he is, can wait until the morning." I dragged my feet, my slippers catching on the loose floorboards as I crossed the verandah, making sure the door latch was firmly in the locked position.

I was curious, despite my tiredness, as to whether Jacob was waiting to talk. I turned towards the kitchen. I wanted to know more. I poured the now lukewarm water from the kettle over the peppermint teabag in my mug and sat back at the table.

"Are you still here Jacob?" I asked quietly. "I want to learn more about my family, our family. I didn't know about you, or your side of the family. What do you think we need to work together on?" Spark purred on my lap, not at all concerned about my newly discovered relative. Did Jacob mean us to work together as leaders of the gifted community? Was there something else that needed figuring out?

I finished my tea, the page in front of me was blank. I sighed. Whatever knocked over the table managed to scare Jacob away. Was that the intent? "I'm sure he'll return Spark. I need to be patient." I yawned, not sure how I could be so tired and fired up at the same time. "Bedtime," I told my kitten.

I decided to keep the kitchen light on as I turned towards my bedroom. Not scared, more wary; but drained of energy and wide awake. My heart beat so loudly I was sure it must be hurting Spark's ears as he snuggled into my dressing gown. I kept it on, kicking my slippers off as I climbed into my bed.

I stifled a yawn. Spark looked at me, from the middle of my lap where he decided to try for a few hours' sleep. The pillows behind my head were soft, soothing and I was too comfortable to move. Too tired. I picked up the book on the top of the pile on my side table, flicking through the pages without reading any of the words. As I yawned again, I wiggled my shoulders, as my eyelids slowly drooped over my eyes. The light shining from the kitchen and the light on my bedside table assuring me that I was safe. The sound of Spark's purring a lullaby as I let my mind wander.

I was in a forest. Not a sparse Australian bushland, a thick forest of Christmas trees, with tall pine trees, their fresh needle smell energising my senses. It was cold. The cloak I found around my shoulders must have been keeping me warm; that and the boots on my feet. Had I been here before? It felt familiar somehow. I headed for where I knew there was a clearing. The trees parted to reveal a little wooden house. A stack of wood leant against a rusty metal buggy. Smoke uncurled itself from the chimney. I knew someone was in, that they were expecting me. The logic part of my brain was in a fog, I knew I should exercise a degree of caution. My heart overruled my concern, every emotion I possessed convinced me this was as natural as walking into the newspaper office. The person who opened the door greeted me with a lopsided grin that I recognised instantly.

He was taller than me, but not by much. His hair was similar in colour to mine, dark, thick and cut short, business like. His dark eyes were guarded yet welcoming, his aura a mix of green and an unusual amber colour. His clothes suited to the cottage in the woods; brown cowboy jeans, faded as if they'd survived years of work, a dark blue shirt, as faded and worn as the jeans, and dark brown work boots. A thick long jacket hung on a hook by the door, next to the tattered farm hat.

"Jacob."

"Beth."
I followed my cousin inside the wooden cottage.

Chapter 9

The shrill sound of the fire alarm woke me up. My neck throbbed as I straightened myself up, having fallen to one side as I slept. My feet hit the floor before I realised the alarm stopped. Spark looked at me from his position beside me.

"Did you do that?" I asked him, wondering if he somehow triggered the ceiling alarm using magic, to bring me back from my dream. If that's what it was. The clock on my bedside confirmed I'd managed a few hours' sleep, though it was still dark outside.

Through the haze leftover from my dream, I determined Jacob to be as real as me, or Seamus. Instinct told me I could trust most of what he said. Not that he'd provided a lot of detail yet. I wanted to know more, to work out what was real and what was a trick or sleight of hand. Experience told me, or maybe it was intuition, not to second guess what was happening. I needed something to distract me.

Compartmentalising was a skill I learnt back in high school. I shelved my curiosity about Jacob, and even the envelopes which I would need to re-read at some stage. The plan was to get through a normal workday. I didn't begrudge my new leadership role, but it was a challenge to find the time for all the aspects of the role, including inquiries, discussions and conversations with towns people. First priority—to read the development proposals to ensure I was across everything happening at the council and in town. Afterwards I could make time to process the rest.

"I've the feeling these things are linked somehow, Spark." My familiar climbed up so that his furry little face was centimetres from mine. "Kettle on, food for you. Shower, then coffee. I'm not even going to look at Jacob's paper until I get home this afternoon."

True to my word, I walked purposefully to the kitchen, filled the kettle with water from the tap, and tipped some tinned tuna into Spark's little bowl. I marched straight back out to the bathroom, leaving Spark to his breakfast in peace. As I let the warm water wash away the cobwebs, I was grateful for my ability to work through things logically, and for Seamus and his knack of convincing me that everything would work out in the end.

With a placemat placed firmly over Jacob's paper I opened my laptop. There was enough happening around Spirit Town at the moment. I could live with the power outage and the weird weather being attributed to members of our supernatural community, our youth maybe, playing around with their powers and accidentally creating time slips. I knew from the past and personal experience that mistakes occurred when we tried out our abilities. Theft and breaking and entering was different, deliberate, and malicious. It was up to Jon to determine the motive, means, opportunity and guilty party. As mayor I'd like to be able to assure members of the public that there wasn't a crime wave in our village.

"Today I'll focus on the boring administration part of being mayor," I told Spark, who'd jumped up on the table and was sitting on my right. "You know you aren't supposed to be on the table." I admonished him half-heartedly, grateful for my furry friend. He may only be few centimetres high, but he was better than any guard dog for protection.

My electronic calendar confirmed my morning was free of meetings for a change. My afternoon was to be three hours of discussion about future development ideas. *Why couldn't we have the meeting this morning?* At yesterday's meeting no one referred to the follow up meeting today. I'd have time this morning to review the proposals and provide my support or otherwise this afternoon.

My fruit bowl was devoid of fruit, there were only a couple of carrots, and one apple left for Buddy. I made a mental note to duck into the greengrocers at some point during the day. It would mean a drive out to Wynyard Street. I'd told Jan I was going to call out and pick up some cake. Seamus would be happy about that. A meeting free morning was the perfect opportunity to see how the shops were going. After the debacle earlier in the year when the previous mayor nearly managed to demolish the shops my parents left me, I made a point of visiting at least once a week. I didn't like nasty surprises.

Buddy nudged my hand as I reached out to pat him. "You'd be pleased to see me, even if I didn't come bearing gifts." My heart flew lighter every time I was around the family sheep. His white and black wool had thickened a little to compensate for the colder weather. Being a dorper he never actually needed shearing. Luckily. It wasn't a skill I was willing to master, although Seamus assured me it was easier than it looked. I let him eat the carrot from my hand, and half the apple.

Intuition told me to park up behind the newspaper office, so I did. That little niggle, which used to yell before I paid attention; now only had to whisper and I listened. My sixth sense saved me from inconvenience on several occasions. My second sight, one of the other gifts I inherited from my grandmother, was a little more erratic. I was getting better at tuning into my gifts, some days.

"You look like a woman with a lot on her mind," Lexi said with a smile as we arrived at the office door together. "Good morning, my gorgeous little friend," Lexi cooed at Spark. The takeaway cups and paper bags in her hands she quickly deposited on the desk so she could extricate him from his carrier. "One of those cups and bags are for you."

"I assume you mean me, and not my kitten." I smiled at her. "Thanks so much. I've a relatively free morning, so do you want to talk newspaper stuff? I know you have it all under control though." I peeked into the paper bag and confirmed what I suspected was a white chocolate and raspberry muffin.

"There have been some weird emails coming in, asking for advertising space. Three people looking for lost relatives. The families were from this area many years ago and they lost touch. Another person wants to develop their land and ask in the paper if there are any objections. Someone else wants to demolish a building. Let me ring each of them and find out more information. I don't recognise the names; they may be new to town. I'm not entirely sure if some of the questions should go to your other office first."

"That does sound odd, and yes, maybe those enquiries should come over to council. Let me know what you find. If you'd like me to talk to anyone, send me an email with the details." I took a sip from the takeaway cup with my name on it. "Caramel latte, I needed that, thanks! Oh, I know what else I wanted to talk to you about. Pub trivia."

"Is the local pub starting up a comp?" Lexi popped the kitten on the floor and picked up her pen and notepad.

"Sadly no, not that I'm aware of. I was thinking we could run a set of ten trivia questions every Friday. People send in their answers by the end of the weekend for a chance to win a prize. I was thinking a coupon for a coffee and a muffin at Evie's. The paper can afford that, right?"

"Excellent idea! Yes, we can afford it. Question – where are we getting our trivia questions? I'm sure the internet has sites where I can find questions." Lexi answered her own question.

"True, and I have a library in the pantry at home. I can bring in some books and we can find some questions there too. Mum and Dad used to run a similar game many years ago." I could still see them sitting at the kitchen table, poring over their books, finding intriguing and interesting facts for their questions.

"When do you want to start the game?"

"July? Will that give us enough time to get organised?"

"It sure will. Leave it with me. I was thinking the July focus could be wellness in the flu season. We could ask Lara for some tips."

"Brilliant idea, Lexi, go for it."

"I'll keep you updated, now go and do some mayor stuff. Spark and I have it covered here."

I smiled at her as I left my two friends to spend the day having fun, as they always did. Seamus always said I was too serious and needed to lighten up.

"There she is, looking serious as usual." Seamus voice echoed my thoughts.

"Listening in again," I said with a smile.

"No. You look intense, preoccupied. As usual." he countered with a grin. "We never did talk properly yesterday, after Agnes visit. Do you want to talk about it now?" Seamus was such a good friend.

"Yes. But no, not now. There is something else I want to talk to you about, but after work. I need to focus on logic, council stuff for now. I have meetings this afternoon, but are you free after five? I'll shout you dinner at Evie's, unless you have to be somewhere else?"

"Geez, one night I have a couple of drinks with an old mate, and I get grief about it. The only plans I have tonight is dinner, with you. Are we inviting the others, or is it only the two of us?" Seamus ducked in case I decided to launch my laptop bag.

"Why not? If they are free. I do feel bad about missing lunch yesterday. Anyway, enough about that. I'm determined to think only about things related to my actual paid job today." I unlocked the door and held it open for Seamus. I knew he liked to open it for me, and I always tried to beat him to it. It was an ongoing joke between us, since back in high school when he would carry my books, and I would insist on carrying his.

"If I have any official mayor stuff you need to know about, I'll let you know," he replied with an imaginary tip of his hat.

SO MUCH HAPPENED SINCE yesterday, I wanted to regain control of the energy in the space. I started in the front office, where there was a couple of visitor chairs and the table where clients could leave a written message for me to get back to them. I dragged the chairs around, so they faced each other, with a tiny side table in between. I shook the cushions of each chair, dislodging any stagnant energy and plumped them as I replaced them on the chair.

Makayla, the council receptionist, stuck her head around the door. Young, pretty, not long out of university, with an air of eager enthusiasm. The black pants suit corporate look made her appear even younger. "Is everything all right in here?"

"Makayla, hi. Do we have a vacuum cleaner I could borrow?"

"Our offices are vacuumed every night, after work," she responded. "I could vacuum in here for you, I do have the keys for the cleaner's cupboard. Are you unhappy with their work?"

"No, sorry, I didn't mean that it was dirty or anything, sometimes I get into re-arranging mode, it's the control freak in me. Do you mind if I reorganise the furniture?" A little guilty that I didn't think to ask her first, and that it sounded like I wasn't happy with the level of cleaning.

"Go for it, if you want to," Makayla replied. "I've a few jars I use as vases from time to time. The geraniums are flowering out the back. I can cut you some and bring in a couple of vases."

"You read my mind. I was about to hunt around for something I could use for a vase. One in here on the side table would be amazing. A second in my office on the cupboards by the door if there are enough flowers for two, please and thank you."

Satisfied that the client waiting area seemed lighter, and with the promise of flowers arriving soon, I entered my office proper. I knew Makayla offered tea and coffee to clients who were waiting, and I couldn't think of anything else in terms of the initial experience in the office. I suspected the last mayor didn't spend a lot of time on how the office looked or the customer experience. Mum and Dad used to collect artwork from local artists. I could bring a couple of the paintings in and hang on the wall in the foyer too. I sent myself a text so I wouldn't forget. Apples and carrots too. As long as I checked my messages. Maybe I should set an alarm to make time before dinner.

"Mayor stuff," I muttered, looking around my office. I moved the client chairs away from my desk, back under the table. I shuffled the table over closer to the row of cupboards, leaving room to walk around my desk. The cupboards were empty since Max stripped everything from the room when he departed abruptly. My records were kept electronically or locked in the filing cabinet beside the cupboards. I inspected the tops of the furniture. Makayla was right, no dust lurked there. "Does the cleaner have a security clearance?" I said aloud to no one in particular. I wasn't being paranoid, just cautious. The bars on the windows looked solid enough. I shook them with my right hand. "Yep, solid."

The strap of my laptop bag dug into my shoulder, reminding me I hadn't yet set up my computer for the day. I took it off my shoulder and pulled out my laptop, plugging the cord into the power socket Max installed on the side of the desk.

Makayla popped her head around the door. "Would you like a cup of coffee? I boiled the jug and made you one anyway." She smiled, holding out a black mug full of dark liquid. "A little bit of milk and no sugar, right?"

"Thank you, Makayla. Great memory. I was about to make myself one." I smiled at the council receptionist.

"I've had a few enquiries about what your plans are for the village, in terms of developments and long-term plans. I politely told each person that they need to contact you and ask you themselves. I doubt they will. I did take note of their names and contact details. I figured you'd want to contact them yourself." She looked a little unsure of herself. "I mean, you took charge before the festival and made sure everyone knew what was going on. I thought you'd want to talk to anyone with questions." Her voice faded a little, as if she worried she'd over stepped.

"You're spot on. That personal contact is the best option. If there are enough people with questions, we can hold a more formal meeting. Send me a list please, who and what they asked." I sipped the coffee. "The best coffee. Thanks."

"I'll email that list, as soon as I get back to my desk." She waved as she hurried out the door.

I sat in the chair I'd bought in from home when I won the election, unopposed. Max had taken the ergonomic contraption he called a chair. I'd opted for the chair Dad used at his desk when he was writing or marking papers. It was old and built to last. Made of black leather, hand sewn, or at least hand made with an upholstery machine rather than factory made. Individual. Ornate. Elegant. Just not very comfortable. Which was okay, I didn't require comfort at work.

I read through my emails as I sipped the coffee. I could've easily made my own from the coffee machine, but it was awfully nice of Makayla to make the effort.

My mayor emails were on a separate server to those I received via the newspaper and my personal emails. It was a little annoying keeping track of all three systems, but I was getting better at it as the days went on. Ten unread emails. I was surprised, some days there are at least twice that to wade through.

Emails from residents, asking about planning permission for building a shed, about keeping chickens in their backyard, and asking for clarification on council initiatives. A couple of requests for meetings to discuss their ideas. Since becoming mayor I'd taken the time to write back to each email in person. I could've asked someone else, Makayla to respond on my behalf, but that wasn't how I rolled. Greg and Kim, two council members both cleared from the allegations of corruption that freed up seats on the council, set up regular meeting invites, so I could plan ahead, noting ad hoc and unexpected chats that couldn't be planned for.

The email from Makayla was there too. She listed five client enquiries.

What were my long-term plans for the village? What developments have been approved? How do we submit developments? What was I doing about the increased crime rate? What was I doing about the gifted in the community?

All good questions, although the last two might take some time and effort for me to formulate a proper response. I decided to tackle the easy one first. *How do people submit developments?* I opened the internet and looked at our council website. The front page said, in bold writing – *work in progress* – nothing else. No options for clicking on anything else. I stood up and strode out to the front desk where Makayla was typing away on her keyboard. She jumped, startled as I approached.

"I didn't mean to disturb you," I began.

"Not at all," she assured me. "How can I help?"

"I'm embarrassed to say I have only recently interrogated our council website. I was trying to find some information a resident was searching for. I don't suppose you know how to find anything or who to ask to finish setting it up? Have you ever made webpages before?" I stopped; not entirely sure this was within her job description.

"This is one of the tasks I was employed to do, but then Max said to stop working on it. He didn't say why but I suspected he didn't want people asking difficult questions. He tended to ignore customer enquiries and feedback. I've created websites before, from scratch. I created one at the last council I worked at." She beamed, clearly proud of her past achievements.

"I must have a look at that one. In the meantime, please make it a priority to fix ours – create a professional website for our council. I assume we have current application forms and information sheets you send out to residents who request them."

"I sure do. I already have most of the work done, in development. Pages for the different arms of the council, waste, building developments, the pool, the library; it's all there in draft. I was hoping Max would approve it all. He never did. I can send you a link if you like." Her face lit up. Her vibrant energy was contagious.

"How about you have one final look through and send me a link when you have it ready to go live and I'll review and approve it," I suggested.

"Yes of course I can do that. Is the end of the week, okay? I have a few tasks for the other councillors I must complete. Or I can drop their work and make this a priority." Her words tripped over each other, excited at the new project.

"The end of the week is fine. Also, can you schedule in a time for us to have a chat? I'd like to know what your key tasks are, any efficiencies and improvements you suggest we could make around here. I meant to have that discussion earlier. Apologies, it's taken me longer than I thought to get my head around everything around here." Makayla's attention to detail was evident, flowers in a vase stood on the table by the window. Pamphlets on the table showed off our little village. Even her desk was immaculate. A jar with pens, a pad of paper, a ruler, stapler, hole punch all one the left-hand side of her computer. The other side was her water bottle and her coffee mug. Her water bottle was one of those large metal bottles you could fill with ice cubes and the water would stay cold all day. It was a dusty pink colour. Her mug was similar in colour, with gold sparkly stars all over it. One of those pretty mugs I always admired but didn't suit me at all.

Before we could continue the conversation, the phone on Makayla's desk rang. I waved and left her to talk and headed back to my office. Those questions weren't going to answer themselves. An eleventh email was waiting for me, entitled: Proposed Development.

We are a group of businessmen hoping to bring business into Spirit Town. We propose a development of ten office suites, in a complex that will include some speciality shops. The ideal site for us is the site in Wynyard Street currently occupied by five small businesses. This development would be hugely beneficial to your town.

It was signed simply *B MacLeod.*

What was with developers wanting to develop that site? I slammed my laptop shut, then opened it again. There were plenty of other sites in Spirit Town that could be used instead. I quickly drafted an email back that gave some other options instead of the site of my parent's shops. Something told me not to press send on the email. I saved it as a draft.

Only a little after 9 in the morning, the perfect time for an excursion to Wynyard Street. I doubted the shop owners who have been served with eviction notices as happened last time, but just in case, I decided it timely to visit. It would give me a chance to pick up cake and some fruit and vegetables.

Smiling as I drove up to the shops. Memories of helping Dad paint the outside, to brighten up the dull façade of the sixties-built shopfronts danced in front of me. The pastel colours, faded now, were still a testament to the positive influence my parents had in the community. Or so I thought. I called into the laundrette first, to say hello to Tanya. She managed the store for me, her tribe of children helping, for pocket money. At only a few years older than me, her short hair today was bright green, I envied her confidence, she didn't apologise for her wacky sense of self. Brett was in the convenience store today, Jan at the green grocers. Were they a couple? I could never tell, but at nearly twice my age I applauded their sense of fun and adventure. When they took off in their caravan to see the country, others in the community stepped in to help. After I'd bought more fruit, veg, cakes and some other groceries that caught my eye, I popped in to see Mary. She was busy repairing some jeans. Mum's decision to open the seamstress shop had proven popular. Lots of residents too busy to mend their own clothes. The wood shop wasn't open—Jim's sign said he'd be back in ten minutes.

"How's the new job?" Tanya followed me to my car. Mary, Jan and Brett hovered behind her.

I dumped my grocery bag in the car and turned around. "It's interesting, the problem is I don't get as much free time to visit and chat with everyone. What's news over here?" The perfect opening to see if these guys had heard anything about the development proposal.

Jan looked nervously at the others and stepped forward. "There's gossip that someone is planning to develop the site, but we don't believe it. We know you'd tell us if there's anything we need to know." She shrugged. "Other than that, it's been unusually busy over the last few weeks, which is good for us. New people in town, living over this side, are grabbing groceries and supplies here on their way to and from work."

I wanted to hug them—Tanya, Mary and Jan, but eyes were watching, I sensed it. Instead, I spoke, quietly, as I wasn't sure how closely I was being observed. My intuition warned me not to mention the email yet. "I'm so glad business is picking up. I've not heard of anything; I would absolutely let you know if I became aware of any formal applications. If anyone tries contacting you directly, please let me know. I'll try to call in later in the week, depending on my meeting schedule."

ON THE DRIVE BACK TO my office I pondered the question - *What were my long-term plans as Mayor?* With nearly two years left of the term Max vacated, when I took on the role, I didn't feel qualified to answer this question yet. I needed to figure out what the town needed, what the people dreamt of. Not corporations and businesses from the city. For me, being mayor was about serving the residents, not making grand plans for the town's future without their opinions and ideas.

The other question raised in the email was a little trickier – why should I want to do anything with the gifted in our community? It was like asking me what I wanted to do about the children, or people who worked in shops, or women. Each of us are so much more than the labels we wear, the jobs we do, our gender or our religion.

Back in my office, I re-read the emails. Using old school tools, a pen and my notepad, I drafted responses to each of the questions.

Three sharp knocks on the door interrupted my train of thought. I looked up to see Greg. There was something off about him, but I didn't know him well enough to make the judgement call over whether I trusted him or not. The police and an independent enquiry confirmed that Greg, Drew and Kim, were above reproach and had not been involved in the Castle Home development business with our previous mayor. At a guess, Greg was about ten years older and a lot heavier than me, his shirt bulged and gaped at each buttonhole. His ruddy complexion and greying hair looked a little dishevelled. One of Spirit Town's football stars in his younger days.

I would have preferred Seamus to be looking after the development section of council, especially after the debacle where the previous mayor snuck through some major developments that were discovered in the nick of time. My sense of integrity, and Seamus's meant that developments stayed with Greg, a councillor for five years. We were both new and wanted our decisions to have a high level of probity and accountability.

Drew, Kim and Jamie followed Greg into my office, none of them waiting to be invited. Which wasn't a problem, I encouraged my open-door policy. Of the five of us, Drew and Kim were relatively new to Spirit Town. Kim used to teach Maths at the local high school. Drew came to town as a paramedic. Jamie and I once learnt the guitar together, as part of the Spirit Festival's elemental music competition for students. A long time ago. He'd gone on to play in a few local bands. I'd stopped playing guitar when I left for university. His receding hairline was hereditary. According to Seamus, Jamie spent most of his time outside on the dairy farm he ran with his brother.

"You saw the email?" Greg got straight to the point. I got the distinct impression that he was a man who was not comfortable with a woman boss. It made him on edge, jumpy, as if he needed to continually prove himself. I wasn't going to let him bully me or push me around.

"I assume you mean the email to develop the Wynyard Street shops. I'd planned to raise it with you at our meeting this afternoon. Do we have clear and concise development application forms that we can send through to B MacLeod? He'll need to fill out the forms and explain in detail why he's certain that section of Wynyard Street is the best option for his development." I waited a couple of seconds for a response, but decided to continue, not giving Greg a chance to respond. "Makayla will have our council website completed by the end of the week. The webpage will include links to all relevant forms and documents." I paused, for what I hoped was dramatic effect. "I, we, need all the information related to this development application. There are other sites that make better business sense, but I'm not the best person to have that conversation with the developer, on the grounds that I own three of the shop fronts. It needs to be noted that allowing the development there will impact the livelihoods of several people. I'll excuse myself from the council vote, but I'll be providing a list of pros and cons from a town perspective first."

It was Jamie who spoke next. "In the past all development applications are discussed at our weekly council meeting. At least they were, until Max changed the process. There used to be significant governance and accountability applied to the applications which preluded the need to excuse individuals. Are you comfortable with me following up with this?"

"Yes. Do you know who B MacLeod is?"

"No. Do you?"

"The name doesn't ring a bell with me either. Once we've all the relevant information we can discuss at the next council meeting. Thanks, Jamie." I watched as the tall man awkwardly shuffled his feet on the spot. "Was there something else?" I enquired.

"A few people have asked me what your plans are. They trust you, I think, but after what Max did, they are curious as to why you nominated for mayor." Beads of sweat were balancing on his forehead. I don't think he was comfortable challenging me. The other three were unusually quiet. I wondered what was being left unsaid.

I nodded, addressing the four people in front of me. "I'm considering holding a town meeting to address this question, and some others that I've heard are being asked about my plans. I'm the newbie here, do you think this is a good plan and if so, who do I ask to set that up? Who do I need to talk to, to get the venue, and the right people there?" I could've done this standing on my head but chose to move gently to win the councillor's trust. "Let's plan to hold the meeting a week tomorrow; so Wednesday evening; to ensure we answer the questions in a timely manner."

Greg, self-appointed leader of the group in front of me, nodded. "Do you have access to Juliet's old files?" Juliet used to run meetings for Max. She wasn't part of his deception, but she left earlier this year after Max ran off, too embarrassed to continue. I'd tried to encourage her to stay. The last I heard from her she was in the city working in a solicitor's office. "I'll send you a link to the file system where she stored the meeting notes. I'll send you a list of who's who; the people we should invite, in addition to whoever is asking you questions as well."

"Thanks, Greg, by the end of today if possible." We were dancing a gentle power play. I was willing to concede in this instance, if he was good for the information. He knew it too.

"Will do, Boss." Half sarcasm, half respect. I was having a hard time figuring him out; his aura certainly wasn't matching his words.

He left, taking the others with him, before I could figure out if I needed to respond.

Chapter 10

After the morning's discussion there was still enough time for lunch before our afternoon council meeting. I sent a text out to Lara, Jon and Seamus.

Café – now?

Not waiting for a response, I slipped my laptop into the bottom drawer and locked it. I shut my door too. Clients could leave a message on the visitor book by the door. As it was intended for.

I stepped through the back door, and nearly ran into a man I didn't recognise. He grunted and pushed past me, disappearing along the corridor. I contemplated following him, but I was hungry. Apart from admonishing him for his rude behaviour, I didn't want to spend time looking for him. He could've been meeting any of the other councillors.

"Hi, Beth." Lara met me as I turned the corner onto the main street. We linked arms and walked to the café. "How's your day so far?" Lara was wearing a crisp green pants suit that suited her blonde hair perfectly.

"Hi, Lara. For a Wednesday my day feels like a Monday." I was being deliberately vague, not wanting to go into details. "Have you been busy?"

"Yes." Lara's vibrant energy was contagious. "I've helped Cliff reorder his stock, and we've worked out our products are different enough and complement each other. We're planning some special offers, and incentives for customers who're keen on exploring healthier options in healthcare. Agnes and I are working on a way to encourage people to buy herbs and natural medicine from my store and offer workshops, demystifying the perception that it's too difficult to switch to plant based supplements. We'll meet with the owners of the magic shop, to make sure we aren't taking their customers."

Jon met us as we reached the café, holding the door open for us. Seamus was noticeably absent and hadn't arrived by the time we'd ordered.

"Is it my imagination or is it quieter in here than normal?" Jon asked.

"A lot of our oldies are on a mini mid-winter holiday coach trip. That Castle Home monstrosity in the city offered a five-night stay, return coach trip and most meals for a ridiculous price. About twenty of our residents decided the offer was too good to refuse." Evie explained as she delivered our ginger beer and hot drinks. "No Seamus today? That's unlike him. I'll bring his over when he arrives."

"Thanks, Evie. He must've gotten caught up in some meeting or other. He likes talking nearly as much as he likes food." I grinned. "Jon, do you've any update? That's not a formal mayor question. I'm curious."

"Fred's still interviewing the people who complained about break ins or unusual activity during the blackouts. It turns out apart from the chemist and newsagents, nothing else was stolen. Gates were opened, doors unlocked, items moved around inside the residences. It is sounding more like a prankster, or a poltergeist. I can't believe I'm considering that as a serious option." Jon shrugged his shoulders. "Your question about whether the disturbances only occurred at homes of those with supernatural abilities, Fred says that's likely, he'll confirm when he's spoken to everyone."

"I'm thinking the poltergeist angle is the right one. Weird things like that keep happening at my place. A ghost is the only thing that makes sense. Possums and frogs can't open doors or gates." I didn't tell Jon about the table being knocked over. It could have been a possum, or an angry ghost.

"Are poltergeists always angry or malicious?" Lara asked, her blue eyes widening as they did when she was worried.

"Sometimes, I guess. They're normally mischievous. Not that I'm an expert." Thankfully Evie brought our lunch over, saving me from sharing my experience with a ghost.

"Still no Seamus? I hope everything's okay; he must be starving. Send him in when you find him, and I'll make him something special." She left three plates of chicken salad on the table, taking the fourth back to the kitchen.

"Great pick, Beth. I love the strong flavours Evie manages with her salads. I believe her parents grow them all fresh in the greenhouse out the back. They must have a green thumb to be able to grow this stuff all year round," Lara spoke, between mouthfuls.

"Or magic" I thought to myself.

"Oi, there you are, girlie! Why did you have to be mayor? Go back to the city where you belong. Leave this place to those who belong and understand the old ways." A man dressed in black jeans and a black shirt lunged through the door, waving a bottle of whisky in our direction. His greying hair was wavy and needed a haircut.

Jon stood up and strode over to the man. "Come on, let's get you home, so you can sleep it off." He reached for the offender's arm, but he wasn't quick enough.

"You can go back to the city too, you and the other policeman. We don't need you, any of you. We can look after ourselves." He glared at me and shook his whisky bottle aggressively.

Jon tried to shepherd the man in black back out the door. The man waved his arms wildly, and tottered back through the door, slamming it shut as he did.

We ate the rest of our salad in silence. I tried not to wonder who that was or why he decided I didn't belong. The more immediate question was where on earth Seamus would be that he passed an opportunity for food. My mobile didn't show any missed calls or messages.

"I'm sure the rest of the day will be uneventful. Seamus will turn up any minute now, looking for food," I said, as we waved to Evie and left the café. The street was eerily quiet as we said our goodbyes.

THE CONFERENCE ROOM table was imposing. More than ten people could comfortably sit at it, without bumping elbows. Enough room behind those seated at the table for others to sit behind, if need be. The first person in the room, I made myself a coffee from the urn Makayla set up on the cupboard on the opposite side of the room to the projector screen. The furniture was all standard government issue. Deep brown polished wood, black trim.

Makayla walked through the door with a box of water bottles; she placed one at each place, where a note pad and pen waited for each participant.

"Thanks, Makayla. Do you set the places for each meeting?" I thought it a waste of her talents, that each member of council should be responsible for their own note taking. I appreciated the personal touch; in this case it's not warranted.

"Max asked me to, and Greg asked for me to continue to do so. I think it's unnecessary. The stationery is in the cupboard for anyone to get if they need it, and most people bring their own laptops, and water bottles." Makayla moved her weight from one foot to the other and back again.

"I agree with you, and I'd prefer you didn't waste your talents on these types of tasks. Let's talk about this when we chat, please book in a time tomorrow. You can see my calendar, choose a time that suits you." I scanned the room, noting the meeting was due to commence soon and no one else was in attendance. Not even Seamus. "If you'll excuse me, I have a call to make before the meeting begins."

"Of course." Makayla left the door open as she left. I heard raised voices in the corridor. I was curious, but more worried about Seamus. My call went through to his voicemail.

Calm, deep breaths, Seamus is fine, he's just busy.

I told myself that it was the extra coffee that was making me jittery. I opened the water bottle nearest me and drank half of in one gulp. The voices grew louder as footsteps indicated that others were at last arriving. Only a few minutes late. Silence fell as the group saw me, seated, waiting for them. Greg, Drew, Kim, Jamie, and Seamus. My friend wasn't happy. I bit my tongue, now wasn't the time to ask why. I tried not to show how relieved I was to see my friend was safe. I waited for the others to sit. The scraping of chair legs and the opening of water bottles the only sounds. Ominous.

Clearly, something was very wrong. I decided to take control, before the meeting was hijacked for whatever reason kept Seamus away from food and put that look on his face. "Welcome, everyone. May I ask that for future meetings, we all try to be on time. Send a quick message if you've competing priorities or are running late. It's a courtesy thing. I'll do the same." I looked at the notes I'd scribbled earlier. "Before I hand the meeting over to the development committee, I wanted to let you know that Makalya will be publishing our council webpage. It'll be live by the end of the week. We can direct initial enquiries to the website, which should make our lives easier. I've received a few questions about what my priorities are and what I'm hoping to achieve as mayor. I was thinking of holding an open meeting in a couple of weeks to address the questions from the wider community. I'm happy to discuss that further, anytime, my door is always open." I expected someone to say something, five pairs of eyes darted around the room, looking everywhere except not one person looked me in the eye. Not even Seamus. I gave it a couple of seconds. "Thanks. Over to you, Greg."

I sipped my coffee, looking at each person who was seated around the table. I didn't know whether I should try reading their minds. Their auras were out of whack, a little dark, as if they'd been arguing, all of them. Still heated, unresolved anger. I didn't like what I saw. Seamus's aura wasn't dark like the others, but it was an odd colour, a little greyer than normal. Something must be worrying him. I scribbled a note to ask him about it later. I turned to pay attention to Greg's voice.

The head of the development committee nodded at me, and then at his laptop. "You'll have seen the email from a B Macleod enquiring about the process to develop the Wynyard Street complex into a suite of offices." Around the table each person nodded briefly, eyes cast to their notepads, their pens scratching the paper. Doodling or taking notes? I was getting a little concerned. What on earth was wrong with everyone?

"I've been made aware that our mayor may have an interest in the company that has applied to develop the shops," Greg continued, his voice rising as Seamus tried to speak over the top of him. It took me a couple of seconds to register the implication of the words.

"Hang on! Stop. Let me get this straight. Why do you believe that I'm involved in some way? Why would I want to ruin what my parents worked so hard for?" Alarm bells were ringing, but I still didn't understand what was going on.

"It seems each member of council, apart from yourself, has received documentation that proves you're behind the plan to develop the area. A plan which will make you extremely rich," Seamus spoke, his voice hoarse and strained. "I've spent the best part of the morning trying to tell my esteemed colleagues that it's all lies. I don't see how the documents we've been provided are proof beyond reasonable doubt, that's you've done anything wrong." He took a deep breath in, and exhaled, slowly. I knew he was trying to keep control and keep his voice as calm as he could. "I'm not sure that the rest of the councillors agree." As he stopped talking, he bumped his bottle. It fell over, knocking his pen into the air. I watched in fascination as it landed on his notepad with a thump. If it wasn't for the look of exasperation on his face, I would have giggled, that he'd managed to channel his energy into his pen. I suspected it was accidental.

"Madam Mayor," Jamie spoke. "We're not accusing you of anything exactly. If you're able to provide evidence to disprove the claims against you, that would be greatly appreciated."

"Am I to be given a copy of the documentation so that I can provide my response against each of the statement of claims?" My head ached, a symphony of heavy metal pounding between my ears.

"Of course. I've prepared a copy for you." Jamie slid an envelope over to me.

I slid the envelope under my notebook. It took every ounce of willpower not to open it there and read the ridiculous accusation levelled against me. I wanted to know who was behind this and why. It sounded like a trick Max would have engineered, but would he be bothered? It wouldn't benefit him. This felt different, heavier, with an element of magic to it. "I'll read this later and provide my response tomorrow. I trust in future you remember I need to be prepared beforehand. Any documents are to be provided to me ahead of meetings. Max may have let the council get away with being disorganised, but I'll not stand for that type of behaviour. We are all professionals. Please proceed with the next item of business." Five pairs of eyes boring into me. Seamus looked worried. The others were more accusatory.

My mobile, which I'd switched to silent before the meeting, vibrated. I slid it to my lap and saw a message from Izzie. Jamie started talking about the other applications, from residents, for garages, pools, a spa and an application for an alpaca farm. Seamus spoke briefly about the agricultural college, and Greg provided some additional information about the distillery. I tried to focus on their words. My head was buzzing with questions. *Who was behind this? Why? What were they trying to discredit me?*

I glanced at Izzie's message. I gripped my hands together to stop the shaking. My stomach tightened. I felt physically ill.

We need to talk. You're in trouble – allegations – can't talk today – how's 5 am tomorrow?

My feet were burning, my legs itchy, as if a hundred mosquitoes attacked me. The previous mayor was rotten, proven without a doubt. I wasn't. What evidence could anyone possibly have fabricated that would make people think I had ulterior motives or was involved with construction or developments? I forced myself to ignore the thumping in my head, the tightening in my chest and listen to what was being said in the room.

"The multiple benefits to Spirit Town, with a top-notch agricultural college, together with the distillery, can't be underestimated. For our youth, of course, but both draw visitors, tourist and students from all over Australia." Jamie's voice sounded far away. I tried concentrating on his words.

"Farming initiatives and innovation in agriculture. That's what Spirit Town should be known for." An interesting comment from Kim, considering she was one of our town's gifted community. I'd no idea what her special skill was. Something to do with academia maybe.

I responded to Izzie.

Yes, 5 am tomorrow my place thanks

I didn't know what else to write. Forcing myself back into the room, Jamie was summing up. Two and a half hours had passed in a heartbeat. "We've agreed to approve most of the applications: sheds, pools and spa, the farming applications, the distillery, and the agricultural college. The last one, the application for the development of Wynyard Street is on hold until our mayor, Beth, can provide her proof against the allegations that she is behind the application." He raised a pile of papers in the air. I hadn't even tried to read my copy during the meeting. I'd no idea what I'd find inside.

Before I could speak, there was a noise in the corridor, and the man from the café burst in. He was followed by a man and a woman, neither of whom has I seen before. They pushed past Makayla. She pulled her hand away from where she'd been holding the door closed. Had they hurt her arm in the scuffle? I looked around for a weapon, in case I needed one. Apart from spare chairs in the corner and a whiteboard, the room didn't contain anything hefty enough to deter the men, should a fight break out.

"She has to go!" The man who'd entered the room first, waved his arms in my general direction. "Her family are no good."

There was no way for me to exit from my position at the table. I would've had to pass past five people, three of whom seemed to have a problem with me. A lesson for next time I chose a seat in a meeting room, not to get trapped. Seamus stood up and turned to face the three, essentially blocking them from getting to where I was sitting on the other side of the table. "Would you like to take a seat and tell me what's wrong?" he asked quietly.

The other two meeting crashers were similar in age to the man in black, the male dressed in dark jeans and a green jumper. The woman wore a long black skirt and a garish red jumper. All three wore the same black boots. Did they step out of the time slip? They looked wrong, out of place, out of time.

The woman stepped forward. The venom in her voice was oozing as she spoke. "Since she became mayor, the door to the past has opened, we've lost power, and now she wants to develop the Wynyard Street shops. Her parents' legacy. Do we even know what her powers can do?" Her voice rose a few octaves as she shook her fist in the air. The two men with her, nodding and mumbling their agreement.

Seamus took a step towards her. "Doreen Forthright. You are powered too! As have your family been for ages. If I remember rightly, it was your brother Ben who turned the main road into rocky road slice and created all kinds of grief to the cars on it at the time!" That incident must have occurred when I lived in the city.

"And you, Tobias, didn't you cause a fuss in the pub when the beer taps mysteriously started pouring expensive whisky?" His voice was firm, but not raised in anger. "Now why don't you sit, and we can chat about it?" As Seamus spoke, Jamie and Drew positioned three chairs for the guests.

"It's not only the gifted," Doreen said as she perched on the edge of a chair. The others sat quietly beside her. "Colin is worried too, and he's as normal as can be. It's bad enough that we have a gifted person as mayor, but her, it makes it worse. You know who her family is." Mumblings of agreement from her partners in crime. "It's all right for you, as her friend, but what about the rest of us?"

"Has Beth ever done anything wrong, to anyone as far as you know?" This time it was Drew who spoke. Another councillor to survive the previous mayor, he was a local farmer, and long-term resident, his family farming onions and garlic for at least two generations. A few years younger than me, and always dressed smartly.

"Well, no, not since that accident when she was a teen." Doreen snorted.

"We all did stupid stuff as teenagers, gifted or not," Jamie responded. "I'm not sure she would step in, as mayor purely with the intent to be a crooked as the last one."

I stood up.

"Thank you, Jamie, and Drew, for giving me the benefit of the doubt. I stepped in as mayor to fill the gap, because no one else nominated. I've no intention of changing anything in Wynyard Street. I take the inheritance from my parents very seriously." I turned so I was directly speaking to the three visitors. "The role of my ancestors is something I have only learnt about this week. I'm afraid for most of my life, I ignored my special abilities and didn't pay enough attention to what was going on around me. That changes now. I've no desire to continue with the role my family occupied on the gifted council." I paused, scribbling on my notepad to give me a few seconds to gather my thoughts. I turned back to Jamie, Greg, Kim, and Drew. "Jamie, we never confirmed your position as deputy mayor. Are you happy to step in temporarily? I'm going to excuse myself from mayoral duties, until you have a chance to set a meeting for me to defend myself against these claims. I'd still like to have the opportunity to address the community concerns, pending the outcome of that meeting of course." I took a deep breath and sat, waiting for Jamie to respond.

"That's for the best. We'll be in touch with a time to continue the discussion. All the information we were provided is in that envelope. Unless Doreen you and your … friends, have any specific allegations against Beth."

None of the guests responded. Doreen stood up, the other two quickly followed. "We are worried, that's all. Didn't want anything horrible to happen, again," she muttered the last part as she led her cronies out the door.

What about the fact that not only my parents, but my grandmother too, were murdered by someone who didn't like obeying the rules?

I wanted to scream out loud. I didn't, and I refused to meet Seamus's gaze, he would've heard my thoughts, I was practically yelling them in my head. Instead, I picked up my laptop, the documents containing the allegations, and my notebook, thankful I hadn't used the one left on the desk for me. I left the pen and the water bottle behind as well. "I'll wait to hear from you," I told Jamie as I left.

Unusually calm, for me, I ignored the energy pulsing through my body. I turned left, towards the front office.

"Are you okay?" I asked Makayla. "Did you get injured? I saw you trying to stop them, and thank you, but please next time don't put yourself in harm's way."

"I'm fine, but thanks for asking. I used to play football with my brothers, so I'm not afraid of a couple of bullies."

I was relieved. And sad. Makayla was someone I'd work well with, like Lexi. "I'm standing down as mayor, until I can refute some claims being aimed at me. We won't be able to meet this week after all. I'd still like you to finish the website. I'll review and approve that link as soon as I can. I'm still keen to know what efficiencies you would recommend."

"Good. Because I've emailed them to you as well." She hopped off her chair and gave me a quick hug. Tears threatened to spill from my eyes, so I nodded as I hurried away to my office.

Making sure my bag contained my laptop, its charger and three envelopes, with a quick look around my office, I walked out briskly, my heels clicking on the wooden floor. I hoped to be returning soon.

"ON A POSITIVE NOTE, it means I'm able to spend some time investigating the allegations, and the mysteries that seems to be surrounding me at the moment."

Lexi stared at me, open mouthed, while Spark tried batting her tongue, as I filled her in on the afternoon's developments.

"That's so unfair! You haven't done anything wrong." Was it wrong to love how indignant Lexi was on my behalf?

"Honestly, it's okay. Whether I'm mayor or not, people have a right to know the truth. Hopefully I'll be back there in no time. If it doesn't work out, I can always come back here." I grinned. "Would you like to help me get to the bottom of it?" I knew the answer before I asked my fellow journalist the question. She was already furiously scribbling notes on her notepad.

"On it, Boss!" Lexi muttered, as she made copious notes. "I don't suppose you can share a lot of the details, sensitive information and all, but if you could give me some hints that would be amazing."

I picked up a red pen from her pen tin on her desk and scribbled the names of those at the meeting today. "I'm going to photocopy the documents in these three folders, so you'll have all the information I have. I don't know myself what I'm looking at yet." As I passed by her chair to copy the documents, Lexi swung around and flung her arms around me. Spark jumped off her lap before she stood. He was standing on his hind legs, his dainty paws batting the bottom part of my leg. After Lexi let me go, I brought my kitten up until he was level with my face. He held out both his front paws, patting my cheeks. The bond between us was amazing. I could never thank Agnes enough for bringing me my little ginger and white familiar.

"What are you going to do with Spark while you meet Seamus at the café?" Lexi asked. I couldn't recall telling her I was meeting anyone at the café after work. "Seamus put the time in your calendar, and your calendar here as well," she explained. "Maybe he thought you would forget, or get caught up in another meeting?"

I looked at Spark. I considered taking him home, give him more time at home alone and see how he fared. It was only 3pm, plenty of time. I frowned. The problem was I didn't want to leave him there, in case Jacob, or someone more malevolent decided to visit. The three people this afternoon would easily fire up a crowd if they'd a mind to. Better to keep him close until this was sorted out. "He'll be okay in his carrier. I suspect he's been too busy with you to have a nap." I grinned.

Lexi looked a little sheepish. "Yeah. I took him out for a walk today too, so he'll be tired. If you're sure, otherwise I could stay back and play with him." Lexi and I agreed to train the kitten how to walk using a leash, like a dog. He took to it quickly, letting us lead him on short walks. Our locals loved it and stopped to pat him and talk to him.

"Thank you. I know you would. Isn't it your mum's birthday?" I didn't normally pay attention to these types of details. "Cake? And Flowers? You mentioned it yesterday." I grinned at her.

Lexi grinned back. "Maybe you should consider becoming a reporter," she joked. "If you don't need me now, I'll pick up the cake and flowers and head out early and surprise her." She looked reluctantly at the notepad, before tucking it into her top drawer, locking it with the key on the lanyard around her neck. "Tomorrow morning first thing I'll help you sort that out." She promised.

My watch told me it was four in the afternoon. I followed Lexi out and shut the door behind us. Spark settled into his carrier, with a sideways glance at me, that said, *thank you, I'm ready for sleep now*. I double checked my bag of fruit and veg. It was sitting on the floor behind my seat.

Before I started my car, I sent Seamus a quick text message.

Café?

The response came through a second later.

Already here.

It didn't surprise me. He'd missed lunch, so he must be starving. I was thankful he'd finally been able to get away from the council office. I couldn't wait to hear any details he could divulge, about why he was missing in action earlier. I suspected he'd been defending the allegations against me.

The café was busy, as usual. Most nights there were specials, often Evie would include 'kids eat free' in the offers. The community supported her café, as she supported them, with wholesome, healthy food, reasonably priced and great customer service. The fairies that helped out were a great draw card. People everywhere tend to be fascinated by fae folk and magic. Winter and middle of the week didn't stop customers meeting at the café for a meal. It was early, but the café was already buzzing with families, couples and singles, enjoying the foods and the atmosphere. I recognised a few people, who waved and smiled. Not in the mood for small talk, still I waved and smiled in return.

A prickly sensation started at the base of my spine. A thousand little pin pricks, slowly climbing their way up to my neck. I resisted the urge to turn around to see who was behind me. My intuition was developing somewhat more quickly than I expected. Not that I know everyone in Spirit Town, it made sense that some faces were unfamiliar. I tried not to stare at those I didn't recognise. Was the uneasy sensation a warning that I shouldn't talk about the recent events, with Seamus, in the cafe? My brain was cartwheeling, as I walked purposefully to where he was standing, chatting to a table of our senior citizens.

"You look peaky dear, are you working too much?" Pearl, the eldest of the crochet club asked with concern. At ninety-five, still with all her faculties intact, she led the group of octogenarians into all sorts of mischief. Earlier in the year their coach trip to the nearby winery caused a fuss, in a positive way. That her eyes were sharp enough to pick my state of mind was, well, mind blowing.

"She probably has one of her migraines." Tannie used to visit Grandma, had known me all my life and then some. Tannie was as tall and broad as Pearl was petite and wispy. Together they made sure the other elderly in the town weren't stuck at home, lost or wanting for anything.

"A little. I think I jarred my neck getting out of bed this morning." I fibbed, knowing Seamus would know it was a lie, but hoping that there were too many people in here for the oldies to pick my misdemeanour. "A coffee and some water and I'll be as right as rain," I said brightly.

Seamus nodded. "Our mayor has the constitution of an ox." He grinned, and so did I.

"He's right," I added. "I'm going to order some food, what would you like?" I turned to Seamus, then turned back to the group. "Please keep chatting to Seamus, we can catch up later."

"By the way dear, we didn't go on that trip, it didn't feel right," Pearl said. "Beryl wouldn't have approved. The others aren't as strong as us. Lured away by the offer of free stuff." She cackled.

I smiled. So many people in the village knew me and my family. Should I ask them about some of the stories I've been hearing?

"I've ordered, thanks, I'll join you soon. We're discussing the pros and cons of cruising versus coach travel," my friend added with a grin. "You never know when I might want to take a holiday."

I joined the line to place my order. Little lights flew around the teenagers in front of me. They were huddled together talking to each other, and didn't notice the sparks flying around them. Young love. I smiled to myself. It wasn't the teens or the oldies who gave me the tingling sense of sinister. The two tables of families with primary school aged children were innocent too. An unusual word, but it popped into my head as I intuitively scanned the café.

Three of the individuals perched on stools at the bench when I arrived, finished their meals and left the building. The remaining customers, four men in business suits, the three elegantly dressed ladies of similar age to myself, I didn't recognise. The others were vaguely familiar.

"Are you ready to order, Beth?" Evie's question penetrated my thoughts.

"Evie, sorry yes, I was miles away, somewhere warm," I joked. "I believe my friend has already placed his order. I'll have a mocha, and I haven't decided on what I want to eat yet." I hastily ran my eyes over the menu board in front of me. It was Wednesday night, and the special chicken burger sounded delicious.

"Seamus has ordered for both of you. He asked me to wait until you arrived to start preparing it. Special chicken burger, a big glass of water, a mocha, and a jug of ginger beer. Option of mud cake for dessert if you guys are still hungry. How does that sound?"

"Marvelous!" I responded. "I supposed he's already paid as well?" I held out my card, hoping to have the chance to pay this time.

"That he has." Evie nodded. "He told me not to accept your money, that if you got here first next time it was your turn to pay. The reserved sign on the table closest to the kitchen is yours. In case you need to talk confidentially."

"Thanks, Evie, you're the best." I assumed she meant if we needed to talk privately about sensitive council business. Maybe we could speak a little about the events of the last twenty-four hours, if we timed it when the food wasn't being served. I made my way to the booth and sat on the leather cushioned seat pad. I leant back briefly on the back of the seat, choosing instead to sit straight up. A habit of mine. Today especially I didn't want to feel comfortable or at ease. Too much was going on. Watching Seamus chat to my grandma's old friends I let my mind wander a little.

I wasn't too worried about the council issue; the investigation would show I'd no involvement with the development application. The strange occurrences at home were more of a concern. The tingling in my temples confirmed for me that these events were linked somehow. The application to demolish my parents' shops, the person leaving the information trails for me at home and at the newspaper, the mysterious Jacob, and the conversation with Agnes. I wouldn't be surprised if the thefts and the blackout were somehow linked as well.

A sharp pain in my left ear, I cringed and looked up, putting my finger on the side of my face just under the offending organ. At the table that held the three men in suits, one remained. He was about my age, with mousy blonde hair cut short, not shaved but not very long either. He eyes stared directly at me. He was reading my mind. Without blinking I raised a curtain, protecting my thoughts from prying eyes. I'm not sure who was more surprised; blondie, who was suddenly shut out of my head, or me, that I could do that. It was instinctive, I hadn't realised I knew how to block people from my thoughts. He jumped as if someone slapped him. I averted my eyes and took my laptop out of the bag I'd slung on the seat next to mine.

When Seamus arrived a few seconds later, he raised his eyebrows and whispered, "That was new."

"A new trick I didn't know I knew," I said wryly. "A lot has happened since this time yesterday." I saw Evie approaching with a tray of food, so I slid my laptop back into its bag. "Thanks for dinner. Next time, I'm paying."

"Only you could thank me and give an ultimatum at the same time." He grinned. "Now let's eat. You may have put up a block to stop someone prying, but I can tell there is stuff you need to tell me, that you can't tell me right now." He took a bite of the burger, while I was still trying to work out whether to use utensils or pick up mine. "Oh, and Jon and Lara are meeting us for dessert, in around an hour."

I nodded and busied myself with trying not to make a mess while eating a burger with my hands. I wasn't worried about residents thinking I was a messy eater, though. There were more important things on my mind.

"Do you think Jon would be able to sweep my home and the office for bugs? Electronic bugs," I added as Seamus nearly choked on the handful of chips he was devouring. He never worried about how it looked when he ploughed on through piles of food. A glance over my shoulder told me blondie left the café. I wasn't convinced it was entirely safe to confide in Seamus though, there were a few stragglers finishing off cups of coffee, whose faces I couldn't place. He deserved a little bit more context to my comment, so I continued quietly, "There have been uninvited guests in both my home and my office. I'll explain the details later, it's a very long story. I've an unusual conversation via parchment paper, with a distant relative of mine, by the name of Jacob. Apparently, my ancestry is colourful to say the least, and me becoming mayor and exploring my supernatural gifts has produced a level of concern for some people."

Seamus placed the last half of his burger back on his plate and looked at me. I couldn't tell if he was waiting to speak or for me to finish what I was saying.

"If you already knew this information, I'm not angry. I've never been interested in the magical side of my family. Agnes told me yesterday, that my parents and my grandmother were like a jury I guess, if people in our town with supernatural gifts behaved badly, they were banished. I knew your dad kept an account of strange events like freak weather conditions, unusual occurrences, as a result of our gifts." It felt odd, but it was about time that I lumped myself in with the gifted folk of our town. "This is more than that." I stopped, needing to process what I'd voiced out loud. I picked up a couple of chips, suddenly starving, and munched them, watching my oldest friend's reaction. He too, remained silent while he polished off the remains of his dinner.

"Yeah, I knew. Your parents asked me not to mention it to you, until the time came when you were curious about the other side of your heritage." He paused. "I didn't know many details about your family. They said it was safer if I didn't."

"Did you know the truth about how they died? I'm not angry if you did."

"There was gossip, but I tried not to listen. For your sake, I didn't want to know and not be able to tell you. "He spoke softly and reached out his hand to touch mine. A simple gesture. "I'm sorry you had to find out like that. It must have been tough."

"It was surreal, but so much else has happened I haven't worked through that yet. I'm curious and determined to get to the bottom of the mystery. All these things are connected, of that I'm certain." My hand warmed to his touch. I tended to shy away from contact with anyone. Keeping everyone at arm's length was easier. Once upon a time we could've been something else, more. That was a lifetime ago. We left our hands connected, enjoying the bond between us.

From my vantage point, with my back to the wall, facing the main part of the café and the front door, I saw Jon and Lara enter. I waved them over, as I quickly polished off my burger. At Seamus' raised eyebrows I simply said, "Hungry." I gulped the rest of my now lukewarm mocha.

Lara slid into the seat beside me, while Jon grabbed the spare seat next to Seamus. As if by magic, Evie appeared with four bowls of mud cake topped with ice cream and a second jug of ginger beer. Two fairies, dressed in bright pink, followed behind her, sprinkling fairy dust over the tables where families sat. The children giggled and pointed at the magical creatures.

"Our friend here, with the bottomless stomach, ordered our desserts before we even started our dinners," I explained. "Sorry about bailing on our meal yesterday, Agnes called in and our chat lasted longer than the lunch break."

"Any excuse for a catch up is good. We missed you yesterday." Lara smiled. "Mud cake and ice cream is a bonus." I knew Lara's views, owning a health food shop and eating at the café. The mystery of how all Evie's food contained health benefits, not matter how much chocolate there was, could be attributed to the fairies. A mystery we were happy not to have to solve. "It's all about balance, and exercise," Lara confirmed. I needed to exercise more, there weren't enough hours in the day.

I glanced around at the empty booths in the café. Only a few people remained eating. None of them were paying us any attention. My own spidey senses calmed a little. I took a deep breath and asked Jon my question, "Would you mind checking my home and office for electronic bugs, listening devices I mean."

I stifled a chuckle at the looks of surprise and horror that flashed on my friends' faces.

"That's not Beth being dramatic," Seamus commented dryly. "It appears she does have a legitimate cause for asking."

"Thanks. I'm right here, you know." I pretended indignance. "I can't give you the whole story right now, but I've had nighttime visitors and confirmation that people may think that now I'm mayor I'm somehow a threat. Because of my underutilised supernatural abilities. Agnes's visit yesterday was to tell me that my grandma and my parents were murdered, by people who disagreed with being banished from our community." I lowered my voice to a whisper, leaning over carefully so as not to land in the ice cream or the mud cake. "It's not nearly dramatic as it sounds, it's been a big couple of days. Now, let's eat this delicious dessert before the ice cream melts." Three pairs of eyes watched as I scooped a large serving with my spoon.

"It's a lot more complicated than our mayor is letting on, and I don't know all the details yet, but it appears we have ourselves another mystery to solve," Seamus quipped, following my lead, tucking into his dessert before the ice cream melted.

The only sounds coming from our booth for the next few minutes were the sounds of spoons scraping bowls clean, and satisfied murmurings about the amazing cooking skills of Evie, her parents and of course the fairies. Evie employed some senior students to serve and help in the kitchen, teaching them valuable cooking skills, if they were interested.

"Is Spark asleep in your car?" Lara asked, in between sips of ginger beer.

The ginger beer was perfect for washing down the rich flavours and textures of the cake. I responded, after draining my glass, "Yes. He'll be fine in there for a while. He had a big day with Lexi."

"I was thinking, if we all go to your place now, we can help you look for, unusual activity and Spark can run around again if he needs to," Lara suggested, looking at the others.

"I have time, and I was going to suggest the same thing," Jon agreed.

"Me too," Seamus added.

"Thanks guys." My heart filled with gratitude that I'd stumbled upon such good friends. "Does anyone want a lift?"

Everyone decided to take their own cars, so they could head home afterwards. My car was closest to the café, having moved it because I didn't want to be too far from Spark. I arrived home first, parking on one side of the double carport, leaving room for the others to park beside and behind me. Dad's dream of a caravan to travel Australia had never been realised, but he built the carport with that in mind.

With the front light on, and the door unlocked, Spark and I went straight to the kitchen to put the kettle on. I glanced sideways at the parchment on the table, not expecting to see any new message, but hoping there would be more words there.

Bedroom table, kitchen table, hallway,

On a hunch, I scribbled a note on the back of a real estate pamphlet.

Can you check the hallway, the bedroom table and the kitchen table?

I held the note up to my friends as they got the door. At the same time, I said conversationally, "Tea, coffee, or something stronger?"

Choruses of coffee met my question. Seamus and Jon nodded they understood my note and peeled off to inspect the hall table and my bedroom table, while Lara and I headed to the kitchen. Lara sat on the floor with Spark gently pouncing on her, chasing the tassels on her scarf.

"It's been busy at the shop," Lara said, as she jingled her scarf for Spark to play with. "I think everyone's looking for cures for the colds and flu that's been going around the village. It's not only the younger ones, but some of our older residents are also seeking immune support."

I appreciated her starting the conversation about something totally unrelated to the current issues. "I'm so glad that you're growing your customer base. It can be tough, getting a business off the ground. Especially as a newbie to town. Not that I think of you as a newcomer. It feels like you've lived here for ages. That we've been friends for ages. Maybe I'll come into the shop this week and grab some supplements. I've run out of my immune support and face cream."

"I'll be there all week, and I open late on Thursdays. Or I can put something together for you and bring to the office." Lara wrapped Spark in her scarf and giggled as he unwound himself.

Jon entered the kitchen, holding up two tiny electronic devices, with his fingers to his lips.

"Lara, would you mind putting my shopping in the fridge? It's mainly fruit and veg, for me and Buddy, but it's been sitting in my car for a while." I pointed to the green reusable shopping bag I'd dumped on the kitchen bench.

"Sure thing. Would you like me to feed Buddy too?" she asked as she opened the fridge and put the apples, strawberries, pears and carrots in the crisper. She handed me the milk, as the kettle boiled.

I looked at the little wooden clock. Years ago, a cuckoo used to pop in and out of the tiny door. The cuckoo disappeared long ago. We suspected Giggles, our cat at the time, chased it and taken the minute wooden bird. "Thanks, but not this late at night. I'll take his food out early in the morning. This cold weather he tucks himself up in his shelter as soon as it's dark."

"Sensible. I often feel like doing that. Then I remind myself I couldn't possibly go to bed at five in the evening. I'd be wide awake again by three in the morning," Lara said with a smile. "I'll leave a carrot and apple out, so it's not too cold for him. Did you know you had chocolate in this bag as well? And cake. Do you want the chocolate in the fridge?"

"Yes please. Out of sight, out of mind." I carried the four mugs of coffee to the kitchen table. Jon was lying underneath the table; I could see the tiny wire in his hand as he carefully detangled a device from where the table leg met the wooden top. I made a lot of noise, shaking the few items on the table, checking for unwanted ears. Nothing fell out onto the table, as I shuffled the papers into a pile, making room for the cake.

Jon picked up a glass from the sink and filled it with warm water from the tap. He popped the three little black items into the water.

Seamus came into the kitchen with empty hands. "I replaced the lightbulbs in your parents and grandmas' room. There was one remaining bulb, so there's a new one in your room too." His eyes widened as he caught sight of the cake on the table. "Are we hungry after that big meal?"

"Thanks, Seamus. Not hungry, but I promised you cake. I'll buy some more bulbs and stick them in the cupboard under the sink, just in case. Do you think I need to worry about anything else, after the blackout?" I asked aloud, pointing at the piece of paper in the middle of the table.

I don't think so. But be careful.

Jon and Lara looked a little surprised.

I motioned for everyone to sit. I pointed again to the parchment paper that I'd placed on top of the pile of paperwork. "I've a relative who communicates a little unconventionally. We've only recently met," I explained. "He tells me there are some people who aren't happy that I've decided to become mayor." I glanced at the paper.

We'll talk later

Intuitively I knew Jacob's comment meant he was leaving me to talk to my friends. Did that mean he thought it was safe to speak freely? I let my senses scour the building.

Another new skill? Seamus's voice was in my head. He looked as surprised as I did at this new turn of events.

"Thanks guys. The three devices you found, indicates my cousin is right and there is someone who's not happy with me becoming mayor. I'd be worried about my laptop and my mobile being bugged, or tapped or whatever it is, but I always have them with me."

"Don't you leave them in the kitchen overnight?" Seamus asked.

"May I've a look at your laptop and your phone?" Lara asked. "I used to hack computer systems and listen in to conversations on mobiles. I had a colourful teenage hood." She shrugged.

"Sure." I passed her my laptop and my mobile. I picked up Spark, comforted by his presence at our table. I didn't sit him on the table, but let him knead my black trousers, as he snuggled in for a five-minute rest. I'd have to brush the fluff off afterwards, but tonight, I didn't care about such trivial things.

"There are a couple of weird apps. One is tracking you via your phone. I deleted it and placed a stronger antivirus protection on your mobile." I stared at my quiet friend in admiration, as she passed my phone back. So many secrets revealed in less than twenty-four hours.

"I'd no idea that was even possible, anti-virus on a mobile," I said in wonder.

"Your laptop hasn't got a tracker or a bug, but someone has cloned it recently." Lara said a few minutes later. We'd all watched in quiet fascination as she did her thing on the computer. Drinking our hot drinks in silence.

Seamus cut several slices of cake, taking a piece for himself. I wasn't hungry, but the cake on my plate gave me something tangible to focus on.

"That means they have taken a copy of whatever was on it?" Jon's statement was more of a question.

"Yes. It looks like only your personal stuff. They didn't try to clone the council drive, or anything from the newspaper, from what I can see." Lara passed my laptop back.

I stood, picking Spark up off my lap. I started pacing back and forth, towards the library and back to the table.

"She's either deep in thought or the coffee's kicked in." I heard Seamus's voice through a thick veil of questions.

"Thinking," I muttered. "Jacob told me, and Agnes too. They, whoever they are, want to know what I know about them. Not official council business, or even newspaper articles, but what I research and work on in my own time. Gifted community council business. My family are judge, jury and banishers. At least they were, until they were killed. I was safe when I didn't believe or use my gifts. Now that I'm in a position of power in the town they want to know if I'm following in the footsteps of my ancestors. If I'm a threat." Did I sound like a mad woman? Would my friends gently suggest that I visit our local doctor? I didn't think so. Even though Lara and Jon weren't gifted, they'd seen enough to know that magic, and good and bad, did exist side by side in our village.

I opened the dark blue wooden door that led to the library. Not sure what I thought I'd find, I pulled the cord that turned on the light, then turned it off again. If there were answers amongst my parents' books, I'd donated a good amount of them to the op shop a year or so ago. The books I'd collected were unlikely to provide any answers.

"Who is Jacob? And how and when did he and Agnes tell you this information?" Jon took out the notepad from the top pocket of his jacket. "I've been busy with the increased criminal activity in the town, but I'd no idea about all this. I would've made time for you."

"I know you would've and thank you. Agnes told me about my parents and my grandma yesterday, about their murders. That's why I missed lunch. She called into my office as I was leaving." I opened the cupboard door, hoping to find some biscuits I had forgotten about. Not normally so hungry, did my increased powers cause hunger pains? "Ah ha!" I found the packet of chocolate biscuits I was going to take to work later in the week, to add to the table for the weekly council meeting. "Does anyone want a biscuit?" I opened the packet and placed it in the middle of the table, next to the parchment.

"Jacob?" Jon gently prompted, as he reached for a biscuit and handed the packet to Lara. The cake that I'd bought for Seamus, sat next to the parchment on the other side. I'd forgotten it when I was looking for biscuits. Maybe I was losing the plot after all. Problem is, this wasn't something a doctor could help with. The embarrassment rose in my cheeks, as I took a biscuit and a piece of cake. I wasn't working for the next couple of days, maybe I could walk off the extra calories then.

"Last night, I was sitting here, laptop and a blank piece of paper in front of me. I was hoping for inspiration or answers about my family. You know about the package I received here over the weekend, with photos and papers, lists of local events?" I honestly couldn't recall if I'd told Lara and Jon about the parcel that arrived on the verandah. "Envelopes with similar information arrived at the newspaper office and my office at council. Agnes warned me that not everything I read is true. I sat here, hoping to hear my intuition, or maybe Grandma." I paused, thinking how much easier this would've been if Grandma, Mum or Dad were alive. "Flowery handwritten words appeared on the paper. I heard the voice associated with the writing, as weird as it sounds, as if he was over my shoulder, though of course there was no one there. He, Jacob, is a relative of mine. I don't think he's a ghost exactly. He was telling me about my ancestors, when there was a noise outside. Something, likely a possum, knocked over the table out the front. When I came back into the kitchen, Jacob was gone." I picked up the paper, and turned it over, was I hoping for a clue? Seamus held out his hand, examined the paper and handed it to Jon.

"I didn't think to take a photo, each time the writing appeared, but the essence of it is that Jacob is somehow related to me. My line goes back to a time when there were both male and female offspring. For whatever reason, there was a falling out and here we are."

"Do you think Jacob was the one who broke in?" Lara asked.

"I'm not sure yet," I answered truthfully. "I mean, he was here in some form, a ghost maybe, but my intuition tells me it's something else."

"Do you think this is related to the parcel on your doorstep?" Seamus wondered aloud.

"I think so. Lexi received a package that explained in detail how my parents and grandmother actually died."

"Jon and I checked all the rooms, including the paperwork, photographs, and the box in the dining room. We couldn't find any evidence of listening devices." Seamus stood up and started pacing.

"Oh, sit down, I know you're worried but don't be," I said, pretending to be cranky. "My magic abilities seem to be strengthening, and I'm finding I have abilities I didn't know about. I'm perfectly safe here. Thanks though." I didn't mean to sound harxh.

"So now you know what I'm thinking?" Seamus sounded cranky, but he did stop pacing and picked up a biscuit.

"Yes, as it happens. I know when other people are trying to read my mind, gifted people. I can block them too. I may be able to travel back and forth in time, but that's a little bumpy at the moment. My energy is pulled into the past at random. Not always at the same instant as the time slips. I get little glimpses into the past of our town, and my ancestors."

Before Seamus could voice the worry I saw so clearly in his aura I offered, "More coffee? Or green tea?"

Jon's mobile rang. "Thanks, but I'd better go. I'm supposed to be at the station. I'll ring tomorrow. If anyone tries to break in, call me. Doesn't matter how late. Thanks for this evening, everyone." Jon waved his free hand as he left, his mobile up to his ear, listening to the voice on the other end of the phone.

"I hope the call is someone asking for help to unlock their car and not about another break in," Lara mused, echoing my thoughts. "I'd better head home too if you don't mind." Lara handed my kitten back to me. He snuck back into her lap when I was pacing the room earlier.

"Thanks, Lara." I gave my friend a quick hug. I turned to Seamus. "I'll be fine, honestly. You don't have to hang around."

Seamus, hands in the pockets of his blue hoodie, shook his head in frustration. "Would you tell us if you were worried about being alone?"

I considered the question. The old me, needing to be in control all the time, would never admit I was wrong. Now though? "I'm not sure, but I'll be okay. I'm going to read through some of the papers we found on the weekend and make some notes. I need to make sense of what I know, and I think reading the documents in the order I received them is key. If I don't get through it all tonight, Lexi is going to help me tomorrow." I gathered the mugs from the table, placing them in the sink.

"I'll meet you at the newspaper at half seven in the morning." Seamus made it sound like an order. I knew he worried about me.

"I'll text you if there is a problem tonight. Is that okay?" I said with as much softness as I could manage.

"Okay," he said grudgingly. I heard the soft click of the door as he shut it quietly. A few minutes later my phone beeped.

Please lock the door. My eyes filled with tears as I read the text from my best friend. I shook my head, to clear away my emotions. There was work to be done, I could fall apart later.

In the dining room, pages of documents and piles of photographs beckoned to me. Cleaning up after supper could wait until later. Images of people I knew and people who were related to me, or part of the community were calling, tempting me with answers to the many questions whirling around in my brain.

My obsessive-compulsive tendencies needed the piles on the table to be arranged into some sort of order that I could make sense of. The box that arrived on the front porch was big enough for all the photographs; both the photos that came in it, and those Seamus and I found in the chest in the dining room, and in grandma's room. Spark sniffed the box, as I placed it on the floor. The photos from home went in first. I placed a piece of paper from the printer on top. "Makes it easier to know which photos are the new ones," I explained to my furry friend as I laid the rest of the photos on top of the paper. With the lid firmly on the box I slid it over to the door, and into the hallway. "I need to work out which room I want to make my office." I looked around the formal dining room, with the mahogany dining furniture, where Mum and Dad sat playing cards and laughing, drinking whiskey, sherry, or coffee, depending on the time of day and the occasion. "Lots of ghosts."

The tug on my heart strings, ached as I walked into the kitchen. As the kettle boiled, I went over the dilemma in my head. I didn't want to set up my office in one of the bedrooms. Eventually I would have to clear the rooms out and create a fresh space. I wasn't ready yet. The dining room held so many memories, could I concentrate? "Do I move the furniture out?" My heart sunk at the thought. "Maybe I could paint it a lighter colour? It would be easier than taking the wallpaper off the wall." Spark patted the wallpaper, as if confirming my suspicion. "The dining room has the least furniture."

Dragging the sideboard from the side wall to the back wall under the window was easier than I thought. Well loved, old, and well crafted, not too heavy to move. A bookshelf and a filing cabinet would work on the wall vacated by the sideboard, near the door. I half dragged; half pushed the table to the opposite side of the room. Placing one of the dining chairs so that I would be sitting facing out the door, I moved the others off to the side, out of the way. I wrote myself a list.

Filing cabinet, a shelf, another table.

I'd no idea when I'd find the items, but in the meantime, I'd made space to work. I picked up the box of photos. It fitted nicely on the end of the sideboard, once I moved the random items I dumped on it over the last twelve months. I headed back to the kitchen for my coffee, lukewarm, but drinkable. Spark followed me.

I yawned and glanced at my mobile. It was eleven o'clock and I'd been awake since 3 am. "Seeing as I don't have to go into council in the morning, I can read through some of the papers before we meet Lexi," I told Spark as I scooped him up from where he was trying to chase my toes. "Let's try and get some sleep." The front door was latched. I checked and double checked. So was the back door. The windows as well. As I walked past the kitchen table, I glanced at the table. Jacob's paper was blank. Part of me wanted to know more, the rest of me was tired. Hopefully Jacob was happy to wait to chat later.

Chapter 11

I must've nodded off almost immediately, because the next thing I knew I was looking through the window of my newspaper office. Except that it wasn't my office, or my window. The three men in suits from the café were standing at the front counter, talking to a lady who looked vaguely familiar. Tall, with her black hair tied tightly back into a bun and dressed in a business suit. The counter was ornate wood, carved with images of horses and large winged creatures. I squinted through the window, cupping my hands on the glass to see more clearly. The scene changed.

My grandma as a child, no not my grandma, maybe her mother, and her brother? I watched silently as they walked to school along a dirt road that would one day be the road from the main street to the local school in Spirit Town. The house at the other end of Tumble Street had been their childhood home. I remembered the stories, which I guess now were only half true. The inconsistencies made my head hurt, even in my dream state, if that's what this was. The house wasn't there now. Replaced by a charity clothes shop, so no clues to be found there. It's a shame I wasn't living in some ancient ancestral home with an attic or a shed full of mysterious secrets.

Next, I found myself in a dark corner of a park, not our local park. My intuition told me I'd visited the bushland before. I heard raised voices. Teenage voices. The female voice accusing the person she was with of using his abilities for evil intent. He countered that it wasn't him, that he had been set up and would never do that.

I felt Spark's paw on my cheek. I opened my eyes to see his nose about five centimetres from my face. My eyes blinked, adjusting to focus on the pair of eyes so close to mine. It seemed like I'd been asleep for a few minutes, but the time on the clock told me otherwise – 4:35am. During winter the sun didn't peep over the horizon until well after 6am in the depths of the coldest season I tried to roll over, to grab some more sleep, or figure out who the teenagers were in my vision. Spark persisted in patting my cheek, stopping me from closing my eyes. "Why do you want me to wake up now? I don't have to go into work and it's not even 5am yet."

As I spoke the words aloud, I sat up with a jolt. "Izzie's coming at five!" Satisfied that I was awake, Spark jumped nimbly from the bed and headed towards the door. He turned back, to make sure I was following.

"Hang on, let me get dressed at least, and find my slippers." My feet hunted around the floor while I grabbed my daggy purple tracksuit from the end of the bed. "What's your hurry? We have time to boil the kettle before she gets here. Are you hungry, do you need to use the litter box, or is there something else?" My brain was a little groggy and I was having trouble focusing on thoughts in my head. I'd been asleep for what, five hours? Normally I woke and tossed restlessly for most of the night. The dreams, time slips or whatever that was that pulled me in kept me captured. Another world or glimpses of the past?

"Izzie first, I can work out what those messages were, later," I muttered, making a point of not shuffling my feet as I followed my friend to the kitchen.

Making a healthy choice, I dunked a peppermint tea bag into my mug of hot water. Sipping the drink, a refreshing boost of focus and energy replaced the lethargy and brain fog almost instantly. Each door and window remained locked as they were the previous evening. Nothing appeared moved in any of the rooms, apart from the furniture I moved myself.

In the early morning silence, I heard a car door shut. I embraced my old school friend as soon as she reached the top step. Her blonde hair, as long and frizzy as when we'd worked after school, mucking out the stables together, during the phase when we thought we'd become veterinarians. I didn't share her love of basketball, preferring to sit and cheer her on from the sidelines. Our lives had followed similar paths, studying journalism and mixed media at university, working in the city. We kept in touch. Izzie returned first, to care for her ill mother, ultimately choosing to stay.

"Are you okay?" She held me at arm's length, her eyes boring into mine." She wasn't gifted, but her intuition and ability to dig out a story was phenomenal.

"Yeah, been better, but you know me, I'm stubborn."

Izzie bent to pick Spark up as she followed me to the kitchen. She preferred dogs to cats, and preferred animals to most humans. Our shared passion for animals the basis of our friendship so long ago.

"I've made peppermint tea, or would you like chamomile?" Izzie told me years ago herbal teas only until noon, then coffee right up until bedtime, she routine for surviving university. I wasn't sure I'd ever sleep if I followed that regime, but I didn't mind herbal teas either.

"Peppermint's fine." Izzie picked her cup, the one with the dogs on it. She smiled, dogs, cats, horses and birds, we'd both kept our matching cups, bought from our school fete, on the white elephant stall.

"Thanks for coming." I knew her day was busy, from now until way into the night. Her work ethic matched mine. Another reason for our ongoing friendship.

"I wanted to check you were okay. Do you know what is being said about you? I suppose you would." Izzie frowned at me over the top of her mug.

"That I'm somehow responsible for a development application in Wynyard Street to demolish the shops and build a suite of offices? I'm sure there's more, but I've a lot on and only learnt of this yesterday afternoon." I let my familiar up on my lap, it was comforting having him close.

"That's the gist of it. You only became mayor to do the same things our previous mayor did. Do you feel up to talking on the radio?" Izzie held out her arms for Spark. He climbed daintily over the table to her lap. I heard her sigh of contentment.

"Yes, once, I've read through the allegations and have met with council. I've stood myself down, as mayor, until I can prove my innocence. Once that's sorted, I'll host a town meeting, where people can ask me questions. I was going to anyway, but it's even more important now." I glanced at the piece of paper in front of us, but there was no message from Jacob.

"I nominated because no one else would. If someone else wants to step in, I'll resign and go back to the paper. But I won't stand for being threatened or falsely accused of being corrupt."

"There's something else isn't there?" Her eyes said *and don't try to tell me everything else is okay.*

"Yeah. Apparently, my parents and grandma were murdered. And get this, because they were magical royalty or some nonsense. Their bloodline gave them authority to banish magical folk who crossed some line or behaved badly. Turns out some gifted people didn't like that and killed them. Once I decided to take on the role of mayor and embrace my abilities, I may have made myself a target. Oh, and my parents lied to me about other things as well, my maternal line wasn't all female, there used to be male siblings after all."

Izzie's eyes and mouth opened wide in surprise. No words came out; I'd not often seen my friend speechless. I decided not to tell her about the other strange goings on. It'd only worry her.

"That's not for publication, yet. You know the blackouts were a result of teenagers playing around – the time slips too. The police are investigating the thefts; and Mike and Agnes are helping the youth close the time slips. Lexi or I will put some words together and email it, by mid-morning – I'll get Lexi to liaise with you on that, is that ok?"

"Of course! She's great. An asset to the paper, if we weren't such good mates I'd poach her for the station." Izzie grinned, reaching out for a chocolate biscuit from the packet I'd forgotten to return to the cupboard. I copied. I needed the energy. "You sort out what you need to. When you're ready to chat on the air, let me know. I wish I could stay longer, but I've a team meeting to prepare for." Izzie stood up, placing Spark on the floor. As she hugged me, she added, "Ring me anytime, if you need anything. And take care." I shut the door behind my friend, wishing it had been a longer visit. I could've given her more details, but it was best to wait until I could prove what was true.

As I collected cups to wash them, I noticed the parchment was still devoid of words. I hoped to quiz Jacob some more, about the past, and my dreams, but I didn't have time to sit and stare at a blank piece of paper. Spark batted the ball of string Lara left on the floor the previous evening.

"Which is first, my little friend? Do I work out who has the development application in to demolish the shops, or do I look at the papers that arrived on the weekend? The papers came first I guess, and they may hold the clues, if as I suspect it's all linked."

Right track

The words formed as I was talking.

"Good morning, Jacob. I don't suppose you want to give me any more clues, or the whole answer. It'd save me so much time."

Silence. No words appeared. I sighed. "Oh well, it would've been nice, and saved a lot of time, but okay, I'll do it myself."

No new words appeared, having drained my second cup of peppermint tea, I decided it was shower time. The carrot and apple Lara left on the bench reminded me I still needed to feed my sheepy friend.

It was cold and I didn't have to be mayor for the day. Did I wear my jeans? The comfy ones I wear at home, on weekends during the colder months. "No, I can't," I told my reflection. Casual and Beth weren't words I wanted associated during work hours. I compromised with my regular black pants, a purple shirt and black cardigan.

For years, I considered cardigans too casual, likewise jeans or tracksuits. Then I saw a few women in the city, who looked businesslike, corporate, with store bought, not hand knitted, black cardigans. I tried one on in the least exclusive dress shop I could find, and I was impressed I didn't look like a frump. Reluctantly I brought the item, for those days when a jacket wasn't required, but it was cold enough for an extra layer. Surprised it held its shape after washing, I suspected dry cleaning would be a better option. I shrugged the black cardigan on. "It'll be cold outside." I picked up Spark, turned out the light in my room, and headed for the kitchen, curious as to whether my instincts were correct, and Jacob was alive somewhere in my time, or only in the spirit world. No new words on the paper. "I'm sure the answer will reveal itself in due time."

Buddy was pleased to see us. He nudged my hand where I balanced Spark, who, in return, patted Buddy gently on the nose. This kitten could pat noses without his little claws coming out and scratching. "Hey, Buddy, I hope it's not too cold for you out here," I whispered as I held out the carrot. The crunching and munching sound broke the early morning silence. I set Spark on the verandah as I gave Buddy the apple. I stroked Buddy while he munched on the apple.

I shivered. Not from the cold. My spidey senses were going off. The backyard was overgrown. I meant to spend time outside, pruning back the trees and shrubs, there was always something else to do. Looking at the old shoes I slipped on I shrugged. Wet toes I could handle. The idea of the tendrils, the branches and the leaves tickling, touching my back, leaving wet leaf prints on my neck made me shudder. "You two stay here, I won't be long." I tiptoed off the safety of the bottom step, my foot slipping slightly as my shoe hit the first paver stone.

You can do it. No ghosts here, I told myself as I took each step forcefully, my floppy shoes landing on the slippery pavers. I'd helped Dad lay them in my final year at high school. It was the weekend of my friend's eighteenth birthday. I missed her birthday party. Lucky, as lightning struck their house as the festivities continued into the night. Faulty wiring was the official cause. At school the gossips spoke about spells gone wrong. Youthful experimentation.

This garden path, Dad joked about it leading to some secret at the bottom of the garden. I'd laughed at the time. Nothing secretive about my parents, or so I thought. Turns out I was wrong. At the very least, giving them the absolute benefit of the doubt, they lied about my family. It didn't matter whether I wanted to be a part of the supernatural side of our family, they should have trusted me with some, if not all the important pieces of information. Things I might need to know at some point. My heart thumped loudly, making it difficult to swallow. Maybe they'd sat at home waiting, hoping for me to return home, after spending years in the city. So they could share the family secrets with me. A wave of sadness swept over me. We'd never have that conversation now.

"Oh crap." The words fell out of my mouth. My foot caught and I tripped over a branch lying on the handmade path. At the same time, the tendril from the grape vine touched my neck. "Eww!" As I jumped, the fog and damp, early morning mist enveloped me. Things don't normally spook me, but this spontaneous foray into the backyard did. "It's only a branch of a tree," I told myself out loud. My third eye fluttered, an odd sensation. I closed my other eyes to focus on it. Problem was, at that moment I lost balance.

I reached out wildly, my hand grasping one of the heavier branches of the old gum tree seconds before my bottom hit the wet grass. Assessing the damage, which could have been much worse; a cut to my hand where the rough edges of the branch sunk in, and wet feet. The bottoms of my trousers were damp too, but they'd dry. "Stop being such a wimp," I admonished myself. The sound of my voice calmed me. I turned, so Spark and Buddy could see I was okay. Was our block an acre, or half an acre? I should know the answer. Not sure what I expected to find, the rear gate was shut, although the padlock lay on the ground. I picked it up and positioned it back on the gate bolt.

Something drew me back to the gum tree, where I'd tripped. I stood by the branch and closed my eyes again. There was something hidden here. Buried under the ground or in the tree somewhere? Intuition told me both places, which made no sense. The voice in my head persisted. I moved my feet gingerly off the paver where I stood. My toes wriggled as mud seeped into my shoes. I bent and pried the paver up. Fingers encased in dirt and mud, I shivered at the amount of dirt and mud my extremities were experiencing. A small metal tin, half buried, became visible where the paver had sat undisturbed for years. My body creaked as I straightened up. I opened the tiny tin and found a key inside. A similar lock to the back door, straight rod with two prongs at the end. A half flower shape at the other end. Holding the key and the tin tightly, I managed to return the paver to its place in the path.

My intuition had been correct so far, so I looked up. I couldn't believe what I saw. In the branch above my head was another metal box. Not there long enough for the branches to have grown over it, someone went to considerable trouble to hide the box. The remains of a bird's nest draped over it. A couple of dents when the wind whipped the branches, the box painted brown, so it blended in with its' surroundings.

"What on earth are you doing?"

I tensed, my fingers slipped off the branch, my body falling to one side. I hadn't expected to hear my best friend's voice. All my senses focused on the box and getting it out of the tree. I could just about reach it on tip toes. My shoulder landed on the large tree branch that saved me a few moments earlier. "Seamus!" I knew he hadn't meant to creep up on me or scare me. I said a little more softly, "Are you able to reach this box? It appears to be jammed in the branches of the tree?"

My school friend was only a few centimetres taller than I. "What now? Do you have a ladder, or something I can climb up on?" Seamus sounded a little exasperated.

"Will this chair do? I don't know how long it's been out in the weather." I dragged a wooden pine dining chair from the pile of leaves and dirt where it had settled, under a big gum tree. "You sound flustered, what's wrong?"

Seamus positioned the chair under the branch and gingerly put his right foot up on it. He tested it; the chair seemed to hold his weight, despite being cased in years of weather. He leant over the branch and yanked the metal box. After a creak, and tiny twigs flying out of where they lay for who knows how long, Seamus clasped the box firmly in his hands. He handed it to me and descended. "I wanted to check you're okay, we were meant to meet at the office this morning. I messaged, then I rang, and I knocked on your door." He shrugged. "I should have known you'd be in the back garden, in the fog, doing ... what are you doing?"

I reached around and hugged his shoulders. "I'm sorry I didn't mean to worry you. I didn't think. I came outside to feed Buddy. My intuition told me there was something amiss in the garden. I don't know what I expected to see. Apart from the padlock lying on the ground, nothing indicated intruders. I re-padlocked the gate." I pointed to where the lock hung firmly in place on the back gate. "I was thinking about my parents, how they lied to me, or at least didn't tell me the truth. Intuition screamed to stop, right here." I indicated the paver beneath Seamus's feet. "This little box was under the paver. With a key inside. A voice, in my head, told me to look up. I saw the box. I was trying to figure out how to reach it. Then you arrived. You know the rest." I took the key from its box. "I assume this key unlocks the box."

Seamus grabbed the chair with his right hand and took my arm with his other. "Let's unlock that inside. Not that you're clumsy or anything, but I don't want whatever's inside it to fall out and end up in the mud."

"Smart thinking." I allowed him to guide me back inside. I couldn't argue with the logic. I'd seen enough mud and dirt for one day. "I should wash my feet and change my shoes."

He looked me up and down and said with a chuckle, "Maybe wash your hands too. Do we have time for a cuppa before work? What time are you meeting Lexi?"

"I might message her that I'll be a little late this morning." I'd no idea of the time, but the sun peeped above the horizon. Buddy and Spark watched us approach. As Spark led the way back inside, Buddy wandered over to his lean to.

"Those two are an odd couple, but cute," Seamus said. "Now go clean up. I want to know what's in the box I risked life and limb for." He laid the wooden chair to one side of the door and headed for the kettle.

I placed the two boxes carefully on the table and gingerly tiptoed to the bathroom, so as not to traipse too much mud through the house. In our house the washing machine sat in the corner of the kitchen, by the back door. The bathroom sink doubled as a laundry tub and was big enough to soak a pair of jeans, or a pair of shoes. I decided my shoes were safer in the shower for now until I figured out if I wanted to keep them. I quickly washed my hands and used a washer to clean my feet. The cold tiles sent shivers up my legs, so I moved quickly, socks and black boots on my feet a few minutes later.

Two cups of peppermint tea were waiting for me next to the metal box. "Thank you, and for cleaning the floor too. I was going to wipe up after my muddy feet when I came back."

"I know." He shrugged. "I know where you keep the mop. Now, what's in this box?" I noticed Seamus was holding Spark, which was unusual. He looked sheepish. "I asked him to check it was safe, not a bomb or anything to worry about."

I weighed up whether to give my friend a hug, for caring. I decided against it. We were both feeling emotional enough already. "Let's see." I sipped my tea and put the key in the lock of the metal container, turning it gently until I heard a click. I lifted the hinged lid, letting it drop to the back with a clunk. Inside an item was wrapped in an old plastic shopping bag from the local newsagents. Before paper replaced plastic carry bags. Brown packing tape criss-crossed the package.

"Waterproofed."

I nodded in acknowledgement as I carefully removed the tape from the bag. A smaller black box sat inside. Made from wood. Did Dad make it? I removed its lid to reveal a little marble turtle, a blue sapphire brooch and a thumb drive. A note, written in my dad's writing, one word – *Beth*.

Tears sprung to my eyes before I could blink them back. I glanced at Seamus beside me, tears in his eyes too. Closer inspection of the note revealed the numbers 12 08 19 68 23 02 59 Another mystery.

"I recognise the brooch. I used to wear it playing ladies with Grandma. We'd eat scones and drink lemonade on the front porch. Mum always kept this in her jewellery box." I tenderly picked up the brooch, the sapphires glistened and winked at me in the light shining through the window. "The turtle used to sit on Dad's desk." Made of pale green marble, the turtle fitted neatly into the palm of my hand.

I sipped my tea in silence. On the kitchen bench, a tiny statue of buddha with a fat belly sat next to an African violet plant I was trying to grow. It hadn't flowered yet, but Lexi assured me it would be a deep purple when it did. I sat the turtle next to the plant, with the brooch on the other side of the statue.

"Are you going to see what's on the drive?" Seamus asked quietly.

"Not yet," I responded softly. "I'm going to collect up all the papers from the front verandah, the newspaper office and the council. I'll take them into work and read through all of them. Lexi will help. Before you argue, you must go to work, you're the only one I trust in there." I knew it was killing him not to be able to help. I'd feel the same if our situations were reversed. "Are you busy after work? We could meet here and see what's on this." I held up the small thumb drive. The device was not as big as my thumb, and black. A small button, when pressed, opened the lid.

"I'm busy until after six. Sorry I can't get out of it. I promised to meet a couple of mates."

"That's okay. I'll have dinner ready." My idea of getting dinner ready was a couple of microwave dinners. He knew that.

"How about I bring Chinese instead?" He paused. "You can get dessert, ice cream, if you like."

I laughed. "Sounds like a plan. I'll wait and see what's on the drive with you. It'll take most of the day to sort through all this information." I waved the pile of papers in the air.

"Deal. I've got to get to the office for a couple of meetings. I put feelers out, about the development applications, someone must know who's behind it." He patted Spark on his way out the door. "See you tonight."

"Thanks for your help," I called after him as I put the kitten carrier by the door. Spark walked over and jumped in, curling up, waiting to be driven to work. I smiled at him as I closed the door. "Laptop, wallet, phone, charger, papers ..." I listed the items I tucked into my bag. "I'll have to grab some food at the shop." I picked up the thumb drive, tucking it into the pocket of my pants. I wouldn't look at it until tonight as I promised, but I wasn't leaving it at home.

Take the drive with you.

I smiled as I responded to the text.

It's in my pocket

We thought the same, always close, no matter how far away we were physically from each other. Would we ever be more than friends? Not even my intuition would provide the answer to that question. For now, at least it was more than enough just the way it was.

Chapter 12

"Where have you been?" Lexi greeted me with a worried look on her face.

"What's wrong?" I wondered if it was the weather or if there was a full moon on the horizon that was causing everyone to worry about me. Most uncomfortable.

"So, you are okay?" Lexi opened the door to the cat carrier. Our kitten jumped into her arms.

"Yes. I sent you a text that I'd be late." I dumped my bag and the papers on the table in the meeting room. "At least I thought I did." Maybe I'd gotten distracted and forgotten to press send.

"You did, but you're never late." Lexi snuggled Spark, who clearly loved the attention.

"There's something else that's worrying you, my tardiness aside. I know you too well. Spill. No secrets. No matter how bad. Did you get more information about me, my family?" I walked into the kitchenette, opening cupboards until I found a glass. I filled it with tap water, drank the whole lot and refilled the glass.

"Not exactly. I'll send you the emails." I heard her fingers on the keyboards as she taped out the message.

"Okay, but can you tell me too?" I stood behind her, one hand on her shoulder, calming her energy. My heart thumped a little louder, wondering what had spooked my work mate.

Lexi took a deep breath. Her pain and fear shot through me as if someone physically pierced my side. I let go of her shoulder. She turned to me and whispered. "Three emails, from addresses I can't trace. All saying that you can't be trusted. Demanding I print the information that you only became mayor to get some development through. Not exactly threats but threatening nonetheless."

"Oh Lexi. I can promise you, none of that is true." My knees crumbled; it took all my will power to stand. My legs appeared to be made of jelly. How dare they target Lexi? In a split second my sadness and fear switched. I was angry now.

"I know that, Boss," she said, sounding more like her normal self. "But if I don't print anything, they'll say we're in cahoots. If you veto it, they'll say the same. What do we do?"

"We find out who 'they' are. We figure out why they're saying these things; do they think it, or is there an ulterior motive? Talk to Izzie, ask her how she would deal with it, so I'm not the only one giving you advice." I paused, thinking through this latest development. Whoever 'they' were, this was nastier than Max the mayor. This was personal. I couldn't let Lexi get caught up in it. My plans to work here for the day, should I head home and work from there instead? I didn't like the idea of backing down and going into hiding.

"You aren't going to leave me here alone, are you?" Lexi asked, reading my energy, not my thoughts.

"Not at this stage, but depending how this goes, I may have to. To be honest, honesty is always our best defence as an independent paper. What I mean is, we report all the facts, even if something is less than ideal. I've been given several piles of documents. The details on the pages contradict each other. I must work out which pieces of information are truth, and which are lies. I'm going to ask Agnes to come in. I know she frightens you, but she isn't scary once you get to know her. Not so long ago I crossed the road to avoid her."

"She found Spark for you. She can't be all bad," Lexi said grudgingly. "I'll talk to Izzie. She might know how to trace the emails."

"You said the emails felt threatening?" I asked.

"They did," she shivered.

"Then I'd talk to Jon. See if he can trace where the emails came from. If he's busy, ask Lara. She has some experience with technology."

The surprise on Lexi's face mirrored mine the night before.

"Do you need the meeting room? If not, can I have it until lunchtime?"

"It's all yours. You know you can work in your office." Lexi turned back to her computer. Spark sat on his cushion under her desk, listening to the conversation. She was right, but it felt like my actions were more transparent in the conference room.

I shrugged. "I know, but it'll be easier to spread out the papers on the big table. If you don't mind."

Lexi smiled. "Of course I don't. Set up wherever you feel comfortable."

"Thanks. I don't suppose I left any fruit here, or any fruit that's still edible?" I muttered more to myself as I went to refill my glass a third time. Increased intuition made me thirsty.

"I brought in some mandarins and pears. Help yourself," Lexi said, as she picked up her mobile. I heard her talking to Izzie, about the emails and the threats.

I took two pieces of fruit to the meeting room. My mobile rang as I put my hand in my bag to find it. "Hello, Agnes, I was about to ring you. Yes, I see. Do you have time to meet me at the paper office? No, I'm not at council today. Okay, thank you. See you soon."

My brain was swirling. I wasn't particularly surprised that Agnes woke up with the notion to visit me. Also, not a shock that Grandma visited her last night. The timing of it all, was like a huge wave crashing overhead. I closed my eyes for a minute. This heightened my third eye. *A group of people in a circle around a fire. All wearing pointy hats. I watched as three were sent away. I opened my eyes.* I knew it was a metaphor, a coven of witches, a community of supernaturals. Were there other towns like ours? Did they have committees and families that made judgements on behaviours? I understood why we needed a separate court to see matters relating to inappropriate or dangerous use of magic. We needed balance. But why did it have to be my family?

I opened a blank page on my computer and started typing. *Maybe someone who'd been exiled by my family decided to return and seek revenge? Is it a friend of the previous mayor who is making up the lies about me? A power play by a person who wanted to lead?* It would make sense that a gifted person, who'd been exiled, would feel safe returning, seeing as I wasn't interested in continuing the ancient role. *Were they trying to intimidate me? To discredit me?* It wasn't Jacob, but he said there were others in his family who weren't happy with me. *Why was I a threat to them?*

Twenty minutes later when Agnes knocked at the door, I'd written a list of questions I needed to answer to defend myself against the claims of misappropriate behaviour. Finding the truth the best defence I could come up with.

We embraced awkwardly. "A cup of tea?" I knew Agnes only drank dandelion tea, but still I offered.

"You should give it a go. After a while you get used to the bitterness of the brew. It has so many benefits." She walked around me, before sitting at the space I indicated. "I see you've come along since last we met." Considering that was only a few days ago, I took it as a compliment. My powers were increasing. Could Agnes see that in my aura?

"A lot has happened since then. I have some questions, but I'm interested in what you wanted to tell me first. I suspect it might go some way to answering my questions."

"I was only ever supposed to fill in this role temporarily, until you were ready. I'm not of the royal blood line directly. I'm not judge and jury, but I fell into the role of leader, the community needed someone to look up to. The problem is some of the supernatural residents have a gift of blurring the lines. Certain deaths become accidents, not murders. Other incidents and historical events blur. Even family lines can become distorted. Think of it like Chinese whispers. Telling our history becomes difficult. People, if they want to, can tell stories, gossip, lies about certain individuals – these lies become fact."

"Is there a way to reveal the truth? To unblur the lines and see things as they truly are?" Again, I wished I'd paid attention when my parents were alive.

"Yes. It takes bravery. Strength. The ability to stop the time slips. Each time we enter a time slip, history morphs a little." Agnes paused, reached over and shut the door. I hoped Lexi wouldn't be offended.

Agnes continued, "Forget what you know about your family. Read the papers like its fiction and not a truth. That will make sense as you read it. Know that the person making all the noise is one person. Not Jacob. Beryl was clear that Jacob's trying to help."

Agnes's hands, in her lap, were silently knitting, weaving a story. Mesmerised by what I saw, my ears tuned into every word she whispered.

"Beryl, your grandmother, and I watched you with your ancestors last night." The story woven matched the words exactly and mirrored what I'd witnessed the previous evening. *The young man wrongly accused, banished from his family; my ancestors weaving a lie, where only females were born along the family line.*

"Your family were wrong in exiling their own and rewriting history. No murder occurred by your blood, despite what you may read or hear." Agnes pointed to the piles of papers on the table in front of us.

"Do we know who the culprit is, who committed the murder and blamed my ancestor? Or who killed my family?" My anger simmered, like wasps in my stomach, no more like a swarm of angry bees.

"We are close. With your help we can begin to unravel a long web of lies. Layer upon layer of untruths to be pared away." She continued to weave with her hands, this time unwinding in the other direction. It reminded me of Grandma undoing rows of knitting, on the odd occasion she dropped a stitch.

"I thought Mike was working with the teens to close the time slips. At least one is still open, I can feel it. Am I meant to close that last opening, once I solve the mystery?" I was going to add another question, asking how to close the time slip, but I'd bombarded Agnes with so many questions already.

"That answer is one you will figure out when it's time." Agnes stood, indicating our discussion was coming to an end. My old teacher put a lot of faith in me and my abilities. I hoped not to fail her. Less than four months ago, even my intuition was hit and miss. I took confidence that she must see something in me, she didn't tolerate fools.

"Read the documents with a discerning mind. As if you must unravel a mystery and write about it for the paper. Take the emotion out and see what you have left." She frowned. "One more thing. You should exercise caution with all interactions. Don't believe everything you are told." Agnes touched my hand gently, before turning and leaving the room. I heard the front door gently close behind her. My emotions worked overtime, hope, sadness, anxiety, anger swirling around with an underlying calmness and peace. There were people I could trust, and I could get to the bottom of this. I poked my head around, to see how Lexi was going.

"I'm feeling much better now." Lexi smiled from behind her computer. "Izzie is coming to sit with me this afternoon to work out what we are going to report. I mean, we will report the truth, once we figure out what it is. Jon will call in too."

"That's great. Agnes pointed out that some, if not most of the information we have received isn't real. It's simply a story fabricated to be true. She inferred that if I read the information, I may be able to sort out the fact from the lies. So that's what I'm going to do. Is it still okay if I work in here? I'll be gone before Izzie and Jon arrive."

"Let me get you some food, then I will leave you alone." Lexi jumped up, Spark following as she headed to the kitchen.

I made photocopies of all the documents I had, sticking a post-it-note on the printer, advising the printer may run out of paper soon. A couple of seconds later I threw the note away and filled the paper tray myself; it wasn't fair to leave all the work to Lexi.

TEN MINUTES LATER, I munched an apple from the tray of food Lexi brought in, with several piles of paper lay in front of me. The papers that I found on my verandah, copies of my family history as I knew it, the contents from the envelopes sent to the newspaper office and the envelope I found in the mayor's desk, and lastly the papers Jamie handed me yesterday. I quickly skimmed through my family documents; I knew most of it. According to the pages, Grandma was an only child. So was Mum. Dad was an orphan, with no known family. Fiction or fact?

My apple chewed to the core, I eyed the chocolate brownie and the strawberries. A sip of my first coffee of the day was heavenly. Bitter, complementing the brownie's sweetness. A sigh escaped my lips. I clenched my fists, then released them, forcing my muscles to tighten, then relax. I intended to read this like it was fiction.

I picked up the top piece of paper from the first pile. Old, yellowed lined paper, like from an old note pad. The pencil scrawl was faded, difficult to read. A handwritten family tree. My name was easy to see, once I worked out the lines on the page. So were my parents, Madge and Lyle, and my grandmother, Beryl. No middle names in our family tree. As I stared at the words, the other names written on the tree grew blurry. On the line above my grandma's name, I read her parents' names, Susanna and Albert. I rubbed my eyes, curious as to why the other words were so difficult to make out. I closed my eyes, centring my emotions. When I opened my eyes again, the page looked different. Next to my great grandma's name was another. Was Jack her brother? His name appeared on the line reserved for siblings.

Five generations counting myself and Jacob. He was from the line of the brother of my great-grandmother. With the originals as the source documents, I made notes on the photocopies. This family tree read true. Most of the generations there was only one girl born, with this one exception.

In addition to the pages which listed unusual occurrences in our town throughout the sixties and seventies, I found a list of addresses, some local and others with street names and post codes I didn't recognise. I'd google those later. Although the writing was all pencil, some words appeared to stand out. I circled those words on the photocopies.

The next page was titled *Evelyn's roast chicken and apple crumble*. A quick scan, nothing stood out there. I knew that roast chicken and apple crumble were Grandma's favourite foods. My fingers itched to knead the pastry, creating the dessert from scratch as she'd taught me. My fingertips always ended up buttery, with crumbs of sugar clinging to them. I tried to get away with licking them, before rinsing them under warm water.

The last page was lined with numbers. Dates? Birthdays? On the copy I notated those I recognised – birthdays, dates of significance to the town – festivals, end of the school year. I'd read extensively about our town's history back in high school. Written about it too. Some dates just stuck in my brain. The other numbers meant nothing to me; Seamus might know more.

I eyed the rest of the food of the plate, opting for the mandarin first, followed by the cheese and crackers. Sleuthing was hungry work. Lexi knew how to put together an awesome feast platter, or rather a platter of concentration. She thought of everything, even making sure there were water bottles, and water in the urn, a couple of tea bags, coffee bags, and sachets of milk. I glanced at my watch, Izzie and Jon would be meeting with Lexi after lunch sometime. At just after half eleven in the morning, it felt later.

Refusing to think about the way my morning started, I turned back to the piles in front of me. The thumb drive could wait.

The envelope Lexi received was next. There were formal documents, deeds to the shops in Wynyard Street, my home, and the newspaper office. My grandmother's and my parents' birth and death certificates, as well as the coroner's report into their deaths, and the police report into both incidents. I highlighted on the photocopies, those parts that I knew to be untrue. I circled those items my intuition told me were lies. The development applications looked 'real', whatever that meant. I turned the paper over, squinting at the back. There must be a way to tell if it was fraudulent, other than me knowing it. Were there original documents these days, with so much being online? How would I find a hidden clue on a copy of a copy of an original document held somewhere else?

As a child I'd played around with invisible writing. Using a candle and then rubbing over the area with a pencil or crayon to reveal the hidden message. This was the same. While I didn't have the tools, I had my intuition and my magic powers that seemed to grow stronger each day. Focusing on finding the truth, I put the paper on the table and waved my hand over it. My breath caught in my throat as the words blurred. As if a cloud formed between me and the desk. When it cleared, although the development application named me as the applicant, another name formed underneath. I couldn't make out the details.

The next page, a blatant lie, named me as the owner of the five shops in the Wynyard Street complex. It was true I inherited three of the five shops in the complex, but I didn't own all five. Scanning the other papers, there were deeds to other properties I didn't own, and other development applications. I wasn't a lawyer, but I knew these documents weren't factual. My parents will cited our family home, the newspaper office and the three shops on the Wynyard Street. If there'd been another suite of buildings or land passed to me, I'd be aware of it. I'd no desire to develop any buildings or area of Spirit Town or beyond.

Before I could confirm the truth as I had with the application form, Lexi knocked.

"You can come in." I stood up to open the door.

Lexi leant around the door frame, having opened it before I got there. "Jon and Izzie are here. I hate doing this, but can we borrow the room?"

"Of course you can." I smiled at Lexi. "You didn't cause any of this, and you're helping me try to sort it all out. Just let me gather up my mess and I'll be out of your hair. I'll be at home if you need anything." As I scooped up the papers into my laptop bag, a hand lay gently on my shoulder. I paused and was enveloped into a huge Izzie hug.

"Don't worry about a thing," she said, with her arms still wrapped around me. "We've got this."

I wriggled a little, reluctantly loosening our embrace. Izzie let go, giving me a smile confirming she was on my side and that everything would be okay. "Thanks," I squeaked, momentarily lost for words.

"I haven't forgotten about your intruder." Jon's voice conveyed concern. "I'll call in after we finish here."

"Thanks." I seemed to have lost the ability to talk in full sentences. Even though they weren't hurrying me up, I quickly scooped up everything and left them to the room. I smiled at Lexi as I disappeared into the kitchen to drop off the empty plate and coffee mug.

"I'll ring you later," she promised.

I nearly suggested it could wait until tomorrow morning. With a lump in my stomach, that wasn't the muffin and the chocolate, I realised that depending on the outcome of their meeting, it might be better if I didn't work out of the office, at least until this was sorted out. Hot tears stung my cheeks as I left via the front door. I knew Lexi was watching me, I couldn't speak or provide any words of encouragement.

Chapter 13

Spark! In my haste to leave the building I'd left him behind. As soon as I dumped my bag in the back seat, his empty carrier stared at me. I swung around to go back into the building. The soft touch of fur tickled me through the thein fabric of my pants. Spark, nudging my leg, making sure I didn't leave without him.

The door of the office slowly closed. "Lexi must have watched to make sure I noticed you. I'm so sorry little guy." I picked him up, nuzzling my nose into his. His loud purr showed he'd forgiven me. I sat in the front seat, with him on my lap. Purring more loudly than my car's engine. Only four blocks from the car park to my driveway. Still, it didn't feel right to have him on my lap, just in case. Spark sensed my thoughts and stepped daintily over the console and put himself into his carrier. The door locked easily, I reached around from my seat, ensuring it was secure.

The events of the last twenty-four hours, the last few days, had taken its toll on me, that's for sure. My hands shook as I backed out of the car park. Concentrating on my breathing as I drove home, to calm the shaking that was threatening to engulf me.

Tap, tap, tap. My fingers on the steering wheel.

Tap, tap, tap. My toes in my shoes.

My tension eased as I arrived home.

A deep breath in, I held it a few seconds and exhaled.

The grey exterior of the house wrapped around a building full of memories. A place where safety was paramount. Wooden frames, lovingly clad and painted, renovated, and lived in for nearly three generations. Was any of it real? Had my mysterious grandfather who died in World War Two built it with his bare hands? Were the stories just that, fiction, or did my parents tell the truth when they shared with me stories of their childhood and family gatherings?

Whatever reason made them keep secrets or kept me from asking about the magical side of my heritage, this was home. Even with the goings on of the last few days. My family loved me and always looked after me. The rest of it, well I'd work it out.

I set Spark on the ground beside me as I gathered my bag and locked the car. He waited patiently. My familiar was good for me. Life took interesting turns and twists when we leant into it and didn't protest. Accepting my skills. Taking a new job. Embracing life.

"I refuse to let it all come crashing down," I told him firmly as he pounced up the steps with me.

My intuition advised caution as I unlocked my door. No immediate signs of forced entry. Nothing out of place. The tingling at the back of my neck told me otherwise. Traces of an unusual energy lingered around the kitchen and the dining room come office. What was the purpose of the visit? A spirit, or a 'normal' intruder? A pounding in my brain – overthinking again!

I rubbed my eyes. Time to focus on part of my life I could control. On autopilot I clicked the button on the kettle. Maybe it was a lack of coffee headache. Coffee and an apple and I'll be fine. "Not being able to get into work this week, mean I'll have time to pick out some office furniture."

Spark mewed approvingly.

"Is there a way to find out whose energy this is?" I asked him. A musty smell, sweat mixed with fried food, a most unpleasant aroma, lingered. I couldn't shake the feeling. I opened the back door, and the front one too, making sure the screens were locked, which I didn't normally do. "Would Grandma have something in her room?" I read the names on the jars on her dresser. A laugh escaped my lips. "Who am I kidding? Did I expect to see powder for finding who trespassed?" There was, however, a jar labelled *Energy Print Powder*.

"So how does this work? Do I sprinkle it or blow it?" I walked into the kitchen with the jar, paying attention to the messages around me. A flicker of light, a flutter like a butterfly wing. I pulled the cork, a little pop sound as it escaped. As I upended the jar a splodge of powder landed on my palm. I picked it up with my left hand and, holding it out in front of me, I sprinkled it in a circle. I blew the rest of the powder off my palm for good measure.

I watched as the myriads of little dust particles fluttered and drifted to the ground, swirling and dancing as they landed on the wooden floorboards. I hoped the magic powder worked, even if my floor was dusty. As I sat the jar back on the shelf in Grandma's room, it must be time for that cuppa. Spark was acting oddly. Dancing in front of me as I walked towards the kitchen.

Finally, I gave in. "What's up little guy?" Spark plopped down, stopping me from taking another step.

A gasp escaped me before I could stop it. Behind Spark, clearly emblazoned on the floorboards, the word *Jacob* written in flowery old English script. My Grandma's handwriting.

"Are you here, Jacob?" I said, firmly but not too loudly. The powdered word didn't look as impressive in the photo I took on my mobile as in real life. A few more snaps for good measure before I swept it up. I wasn't about to leave that mess on the floor.

"Jacob, I'm going to make a cuppa and sit at the table. I'd like to chat, if you have time." Resisting the urge to look at the paper, I busied myself making a cup of coffee. A search of the fridge revealed I needed to go grocery shopping. A few strawberries and half a chocolate bar stared at me, begging me to eat them.

"This will have to do," I told Spark, pouring him a little milk into his bowl. I sat at the table, with my laptop, coffee and snacks. "So, Jacob, you are here? Are you a ghost?"

Not a ghost no. I'm as real as you.

"Then why aren't you here, talking to me in person?"

It's complicated.

"Do you live anywhere near here, in Australia somewhere at least? Can you tell me about your family, our family? What's truth and what isn't?"

Watch the thumb drive

I couldn't believe I'd forgotten the tiny hard drive sitting in my pocket. I sat it on the table. I'd promised Seamus, and although tempted, I wouldn't discover its contents without him.

"Oh, my goodness, tonight! I forgot to get the ice cream." The clock reassured me there was plenty of time. "Before I go, Jacob, do you have anything else you wish to tell me?

Jacob was conspicuous by his absence. After telling me to watch the thumb drive, he went silent.

"You be good, I won't be long." I'd left Spark alone before, and I knew he'd behave, even with the doors to all the rooms now open. Buying dessert for dinner tonight wouldn't take long, but it took my mind off my current dilemma.

So many cars in the car park. I sighed as I wrapped my cardigan around myself. I wasn't cold so much as hoping people wouldn't notice me. Head bowed, I passed a few people, preoccupied with their grocery lists, and their kids. I grasped the basket handle tightly.

"Never grocery shop after school, after work, or when you're hungry," I muttered a piece of advice I heard years ago. A punnet of strawberries and a punnet of raspberries. More carrots for Buddy. Why was the bakery next to the fresh fruit and vegetables? Chocolate caramel mudcake would work with ice cream. While I was there, I grabbed some more food for Spark. Ice cream. Can't forget the ice cream. Chocolate with chocolate chips.

"Beth, is that you?" I swung around to place the voice. I didn't recognise the well-dressed man standing in front of my in the freezer aisle. Not a surprise, I didn't know everybody who lived in Spirit Town.

"Hello, yes my name is Beth." I held out my hand. "I'm sorry but I don't think I know you. Have we met?"

"We haven't met directly, but your reputation precedes you." The well-spoken male somehow sounded condescending.

"I didn't catch your name." I chose to ignore his attitude, but I was curious.

"I didn't provide my name. Are you, as mayor, going to address the allegations being made against you? Are you going to provide an adequate explanation as to why you've submitted development applications through council, and how proposing developments which will enhance your property portfolio is any different to the behaviour of your predecessor?"

His attack was verbal, but more like a physical assault. I took a step back and bumped into the freezer containing the ice cream. A young mother pushing a pram had to step out of the way as I dropped my basket of groceries. The redness and heat in my face grew as anger and embarrassment competed in equal parts. I was still mayor, but beyond that, no matter what secrets my parents chose to keep, I wasn't having their names sullied.

"You're mistaken. I have not and would not submit any kind of application for development or improvement to properties for my own benefit or monetary gain, whilst on council. I suggest you check your facts before trying to defame myself, or anyone in town." A deep breath in, not so big that this stranger would notice, to calm myself. "You, sir, have me at a disadvantage. You clearly know who I am, but I don't know you. May I have your name? I'd like the opportunity to discuss your concerns further. Either privately or in an open forum, where we both have an opportunity to speak."

A crowd was beginning to form around the frozen dessert section. All eyes focused on the altercation between me and this stranger. My energy buzzed and fizzed. I imagined this was the feeling if I had placed my finger in an electrical socket. Not that I understood how someone would voluntarily do that. Four mothers, with children of assorted sizes, I recognised at least one of them as a teacher at the local primary school, stood to one side. A couple of older women, three older men, getting their dinner before it turned colder outside, stopped talking to listen. A few in more formal work attire were wandering over to see what all the fuss was about. Behind me was probably the same, onlookers curious as to the spectacle in the frozen confectionary section.

"What's wrong with discussing this here? Do you need time to confer with your cronies, to get your story straight? The applications are self-explanatory I would have thought. They are public record." As he spoke, I scrutinised this man in front of me. Maybe ten years my senior, though it was difficult to pick his age. His short, dark hair was slicked back with non-greasy hair product; his tanned skin added to the image of sleazy dishonest businessman. His navy suit jacket had a white handkerchief in its pocket, yet he didn't look out of place.

Smoke and mirrors

Humans with extraordinary abilities were able to muddle things. Make things appear different, skew reality. A slight smirk on the face in front of me told me I was spot on, and dealing with someone who could read minds. I raised my defences, realising it may be a little late, but at least now I'd some idea of the abilities of the being I was dealing with.

"We both know official documents can be forged, manipulated, and created falsely. I'd step aside as mayor if our community consensus supports that course of action. I'm asking for the opportunity to address the community. To answer questions from all my constituents. Whatever the outcome of the meeting may be, time will prove I haven't, and am not planning to, submit any applications for development." I handed the stranger a business card. "I invite you to email me your concerns, or alternately ring the council and ask for a meeting, with myself or any other member of council." Without waiting for a response, I picked up my basket, luckily the items had not bounced out when I dropped it and made my way to the checkout.

My heart pounded in my chest. The blood pulsing around my body, hot, angry, flushed.

Calm, you are safe

I made myself focus on each step Even with my cloak of protection around me, the stranger penetrated my wall, and the emotions and questions of the people who witnessed the conversation trailed after me. I couldn't do anything about that now. Best to put together a logical plan of attack going forward. I smiled at the young man who scanned my few items through.

"How has your day been?" he asked automatically.

"Busy." It was my standard response. I didn't feel like elaborating. "How about yours?"

"School. Only just started my shift," he shrugged.

I swiped my card. "Enjoy the rest of your day." I was on autopilot, my brain already trying to work out my next steps. He didn't notice, already scanning through the next lot of groceries on the conveyor. I picked up my bag and left. Normally I looked everyone in the eye, greeted them and shared a smile. This afternoon I kept my eyes averted, watching the paved floor in front of me. I couldn't decide if I wanted the ground to swallow me or not; I suspected my fighting instinct would kick in soon.

The icy air hit me as I exited the shop.

SPARK MET ME AS I OPENED the door. He didn't wait for me to pick him up. Using the grocery bag as a springboard he leapt up onto it and up into my arms. I juggled my keys, my kitten, and the bag as I walked to the kitchen. Luckily, cats have an innate sense of balance. I held myself as straight as I could, with my kitten on my shoulder.

"You know what happened at the shop, don't you?" I crooned putting the grocery bag on the kitchen bench. "I needn't have worried about how you would go by yourself. Turns out it was I who needed a chaperone." He jumped from my shoulder to the bench. Normally I would've shooed him to the floor. Today I let him stay there as I put the ice cream in the freezer and the other groceries away. My phone started buzzing and beeping before I'd closed the refrigerator door.

I sighed.

"Do I ignore it?" I asked aloud. I sat the phone on the bench, picked up Spark and grabbed a carrot from the fridge.

"Hey, Buddy. A special treat for you." I forced myself to relax as Buddy nuzzled my hand. I lowered myself onto the top step, shivering as the cold reached my legs through the fabric of my trousers. Cold, damp, darkness was already starting to seep into the mid-winter days. Matching my mood perfectly, except that I refused to give in to melancholy.

"Do I want to be mayor?" I asked my furry friends. Spark hopped into my lap, and Buddy stood in front of me, listening intently, loving the attention. "I don't care about power, or the notoriety. I stepped up because no one else would. I thought I was doing the right thing. It'd be easier to resign and go back to the paper." After a minute's silence, listening to the air around me, the whispering of the trees, I changed my mind. "Except that it wouldn't be any easier. They've accused me of something that isn't true. No matter what's happening behind the scenes with my family or the gifted in the community I want to, no I must, clear my name. Whether I'm mayor or not at the end of this, I don't really care. As long as whoever is mayor is there for the right reason. It doesn't have to be me."

Patience

I laughed out loud. I did tend to jump right in. To speak and act when I would have been better off waiting.

"Someone is trying to discredit me, to a certain extent, the word is already out there. If I jump right in, it could cause more damage." Buddy and Spark's expressions told me they agreed. "I'm better off making a plan, including an option for a town meeting, if council supports it. Once I have all the facts, and evidence."

Buddy nuzzled my neck. Spark purred from his position on my lap. I took my pets' reactions as approval of my plan.

"Right then." I stood up. Spark barely had time to hop out of the way.

Fifteen missed calls, seven from Seamus, three from Lexi, one each from Jon, Izzie, Lara, and two numbers I didn't recognise. The *beep beep* continued as messages arrived. I sent out a message to all five, that simply said,

I'm okay, home safe.

I added, *Tomorrow morning meeting five am here if you can make it.*

I chose the time knowing Izzie's day started early.

To Seamus only I sent, *we're still on for this evening, I have ice cream and cake.*

Several more beeps. Lexi, Lara, Jon, and Izzie all sent thumbs up.

Seamus' text said, *Good*

Guessing he was referring to the ice cream, I smiled and turned the volume of my phone to silent.

I flipped the light switch in the dining room office, to chase away the late afternoon gloom. "I need to add better lighting to my list," I told Spark. He sat on the floor by my feet as I unpacked the papers from my laptop bag into their piles. A bony finger tapped me on the shoulder. I swung around, but no one was there. I shivered, not cold, had I dragged in some not so pleasant energy with me from the supermarket?

Grandma taught me when I was five, how to click my fingers to change the energy around me. The weak snapping sound as I did wasn't going to be enough. Spark followed as I changed into my comfy purple tracksuit, slipping my patchwork boots onto my feet. He chased my feet as I shuffled into Grandma's room. I opened her wardrobe, immediately locating the item I was looking for. A cardboard box the size of a toaster, full of candles of all sizes, incense sticks and cones. I shook the box of matches, pleased to hear it wasn't empty. I'd misplaced the lighter when I last lit the candle that sat on my bedside table.

In each room, including the bedrooms, I lit a large tea light candle and a stick of the sage incense. Two sticks in my room, the kitchen, and the dining room. I shooed the negative energy out the open front door, ignoring the blast of freezing air that met me.

Banish and be gone!

Negative energy, malevolent spirits, all who have less than noble intent – leave now!

Loudly, boldly, and with a strength that surprised me I banished whatever was hanging around. Both screen doors banged wide open, the entities unlocking them as they exited. I left the solid doors open while I boiled the kettle and set up plates and serving utensils in the kitchen, just to be sure the malevolent spirit was gone.

With my cup of steaming peppermint tea on the table next to my laptop, I retrieved the thumb drive from the pocket of my pants, dumped on my bed earlier, I sat it next to my laptop. The time was dragging. It wasn't even six o'clock yet. I closed both external doors and checked the candles and incense were still lit and nowhere near anything that would catch fire. The table lamp in the hallway set an eerie glow into each of the rooms.

I glanced at the cushion I had put in the corner of the dining room. Spark was busy preening himself, content, so I knew there was no more disruptions to the energy.

A niggling feeling in the back of my brain; what was the missing piece of information? I looked at the thumb drive. Apart from the messages beyond the grave. Intuition told me to google.

Google what?

My fingers sat poised above the keyboard, waiting for inspiration. Grandma and her friends, sitting on the front verandah. They used to eat scones and talk about their gardens. About plants and recipes. Their *Sage Time* they used to call it.

Old Cronies Coven, or *Old Crones Coven.* Dad used to mutter with a smile.

Mum and Dad used to host dinners. The guest list varied. The name of these get-togethers eluded me. Was there a pattern to any of it? Maybe it was all just random; my over tired, overactive imagination jumping at craziness?

Sage meant wisdom, old and wise. Grandma, Agnes, Pearl and Tannie were all wise, not just in the old ways, magic spells, they knew people. "People watching," Grandma used to say, "is a very productive pastime."

I understood her meaning. Watching how people speak, their body language, provided clues to their motivations and emotional state of mind.

I googled witch celebrations. I stared at the screen. I had no idea there were celebrations that honoured the phases of the moon. Or that there was something called the witch wheel – festivals throughout the year, celebrating the harvests and the changing seasons. Did my parents and my grandma host their get togethers to coincide with these natural markers? I bookmarked a couple of the sites that referred to these festivities. Before closing my laptop, I made notes, something to ask Agnes about next time I saw her.

When my mum and dad hosted dinners here, I thought they were catching up with friends or maybe work mates, I didn't take any notice. Especially in high school, when it wasn't cool to spend time with parents and their friends. If I'd known about their additional role as judge, I would have paid more attention to who they spent time with.

Suddenly, I could see the dining room as it must have looked. The long dining room table set for eight. A black and white tablecloth with a bright red and orange table runner. A large vase of roses, a bowl of apples and oranges and a platter of home-made bread positioned in the middle, on the runner. Two silver candelabras, each with three long black taper candles, their flames flickering. Three courses of silver cutlery at each seat. Each handle ornately carved—heavy, not flimsy. Embossed wine glasses at each place setting. One long and thin, the other wider; one for red and one for white. The faces of those gathered were out of focus, their words more whispers, like I had the television muted. Fascinated, the vision was almost real enough to reach out and touch them. Slowly fading, until I was staring at my messy kitchen bench. A sharp knock at the front door jolted me back into reality.

"It's locked. The dinner is getting cold." Seamus' muffled voice came from the other side of the door.

"I dead bolted it, sorry," I greeted Seamus as the welcoming smell of fried rice and an assorted of other dishes reminded me I hadn't eaten for a while. Normally, Seamus just walked in. I'd given him a key; this place his home as much as it was mine.

He raised his eyebrows. "You've been busy. I want to hear about it. Food first. Then the other stuff."

I smiled, grateful that he didn't start with a barrage of questions. There was so much I wanted to say, but that lump in my throat made it difficult to speak. I took the bag and laid the plastic containers out on the kitchen table, which I had cleared, when I'd been setting up plates and utensils earlier.

"I grabbed a bottle of ginger beer." He placed it on the table.

I reached around for a couple of glasses from the bench. "Great idea, thanks. Dinner smells divine. I'd no idea I was hungry, but I am. Did you have a good catch up with your friends?"

"Scott and Mark want to enter the basketball competition. They just need a couple more people. I'm not sure how long my knees will last, but I'm willing to give it a go. Their other option was golf, which would be boring, and it takes so long." He ripped open the lids and shovelled decent servings of everything on both our plates as he spoke.

It was my turn to raise my eyebrows.

"I want to make sure you eat a decent amount," he simply said. "I'm betting you have probably eaten a couple of pieces of fruit, chocolate, and coffee. All day."

I shrugged. "I'm sure I've eaten more than that. I've had peppermint tea too."

"Uh huh. Exactly." He slid one of the plates over to me.

Silence fell as we both tucked into the satay chicken, fried rice, beef in black bean, and sweet and sour pork while it was hot. I paused eating to pour us both some ginger beer. Spark wandered over, rubbed against both our legs, before hopping onto his bed, where he could keep a watchful eye on us. The sound of our forks scraping the plates clean, loud in the quiet space.

"Are you sure you'll be able to fit in cake and ice cream?" I asked as my friend started on a second serving, a smaller portion than before. "On second thought, no answer required."

I felt a little better. The healing power of food. "When I grabbed dessert, at the supermarket, someone accosted me, and in front of a group of people accused me of abusing my power, being like Max. It was all lies, but mud sticks. I got angry and upset. Your voice in my head told me to be patient and calm. The best plan seems to be to get all the facts and hold a public meeting.

In the end if I'm not mayor, that's fine with me, as long as whoever is mayor, is legit and in it for the right reason." I held up my hand, stopping Seamus's comments until I had finished. "Those documents, that I received here, show me my real family history, and not the version my parents shared. There are names, dates, addresses and some old family recipes. Those documents all *feel* true. The papers that Lexi received at the paper are false. Although they look like official documents, they're not real. I haven't submitted development applications; I don't own a lot of real estate. The documents are fake. The account of my parents' deaths and my grandma's deaths seems legit though, from what Lexi can ascertain. The information Jamie handed to me are similar, all doctored to create a false story about me. Agnes confirmed that it is possible to muddle the truth. One of my new abilities allows me to see past the lies in the documents. Jacob suggested the answer is on that thumb drive." I stopped. The rush of energy propelling me to speak had passed. I sipped my drink.

He eyed me over the rim of his glass.

"I've been involved in several meetings today. The councillors aren't ready to hear your side of the story yet, they're still gathering information. We've been approached by a Dean Collier, who provided documents alleging that your investment portfolio is large, that you own a large chunk of land in the area and that you have big development plans. I insisted these documents were falsified. Everyone is still recovering from what Max tried to do to our town, they don't know what to think. Credit to them, none of them thought you were dishonest, but in the light of actual evidence, they don't know what to do. I've asked they give you an opportunity to defend yourself. Can you prove they are false documents?" he asked a little glumly.

"I'm hoping via the thumb drive. I mean, my intuition has shown the documents to be false but unless they're willing to believe in that ..."

"Thumb drive before dessert then?" he suggested.

"I'm so glad you said that." I led the way to the dining room. "My new office." I dragged a second chair next to mine. Spark kneaded the cushion in the corner as I plugged the thumb drive into my laptop.

Three files. One contained a video titled *Watch this first*. Folder two contained *True family history*. Folder three *Official documents*. My heart beat so loudly, Seamus must have been able to hear it. Seamus's fingers slid gently on top of mine as I clicked the video.

My dad's face filled the screen, the sideboard behind him the same as the one in front of me.

If you are watching this, then your mother and I have been murdered. Beth, I'm sorry we were less than truthful. We never lied, but we did keep vital pieces of information from you. Your grandmother was murdered. In a way we were glad you never expressed an interest in the supernatural side of our family. It kept you safe. Keeping the truth from you kept you safe. Please be careful. The family documents will provide the additional details. You're part of a family history that has a leadership role in the gifted community. If people transgress and cause harm, we have the authority to banish them, this isn't always well received. Most people accept their punishment. Occasionally a powerful force comes along who's not happy with the decision. That's how we lost your grandmother and as you watch this now that same thing happened to us. Your mother and I love you, a love that transcends life and death. We're sorry we've left it for you to clean up. If you've decided to investigate or take a more active role in the community, there is likely to be a faction that tries to discredit you. If this occurs, the documents on this drive will prove your innocence. Agnes, Mrs Marigold, will provide you whatever support you need. You can trust her with your life.

As the video picture of my father faded to static, a loud bang outside shook the house.

Chapter 14

Seamus and I shot up and to the front door. I grabbed the umbrella, and Seamus picked up Grandma's walking stick that sat beside it. After a few seconds with no other noise, I opened the door, and we stepped outside.

Nothing was out of place on my verandah, thank goodness. Across the road, a few of the neighbours gathered. A smell of smoke wafted by as the streetlights dropped their light. Any light from inside was extinguished and we were left in total darkness, save for the half-moon that was hiding between the taller eucalypts that lined the street.

"Not another blackout!" Mr Wills exclaimed. Directly across the street, the Wills's family front yard was strewn with old cars. Since he retired, my neighbour helped the car club, making sure their vehicles were mechanically sound.

Seamus tapped my arm at the same time I saw it too. The garage behind Mr Wills had flames licking out from under it. He bolted across the road, yelling out for everyone to move away from the area, as I rang the emergency number.

"Move away from the garage," I told the neighbours, who were frozen in place. I placed my hand on their arms and slowly ushered them away, to the vacant block four doors away. I stood in front of them, as we listened to the high-pitched squeal of sirens getting louder as the fire engine approached.

Seconds later the fire engine arrived and quickly extinguished the blaze. Petrol and paint fumes ignited somehow, according to Mark, our volunteer fireman. No injuries. Mark assured everyone, telling them to go inside, shut their doors and stay warm. Miraculously the fire hadn't spread from the garage.

"I can help you clean up the mess tomorrow," Mark offered Mr Wills, before Seamus or I could offer to help.

Jon arrived as the lights in the street came back to life. "It was unrelated," he confirmed when Seamus mentioned the lights went out when we saw the fire. "Human error. Not magic or time slip related thank goodness."

Did someone light the fire to get us out of the house and away from the thumb drive? Had I locked the front door? I hadn't paid attention to my house with all the goings on in the street.

"I'll be there in the morning," Jon said, noting my distraction.

"Thanks. Sorry, but I want to check everything okay at home." I didn't wait for an answer as I left Seamus and Jon.

SEAMUS INSISTED ON staying the night. He curled up on Grandma's bed. I loved that he was determined to protect me and I really enjoyed his company. However, I didn't need anyone to guard me, not even my best friend in the whole world. But after the stress of the fire, tiredness overruled my stubbornness. I didn't argue, much. Spark jumped up on the bed with him. "It's not like the fire was here. Anything could have started it. It could've been an accident." I rolled my eyes.

The minutes slowly ticked by. By 2am I decided enough was enough. The light on my bedside was enough to read by. The pile of books beside my bed beckoned. I skim read a book about a family who left the city to travel the world, in a boat. A big boat. I'd be claustrophobic in the first week.

I heard footsteps as Seamus crossed the hall. "Are you awake?"

"No," I answered with a smile.

"Then I guess you don't want a coffee, and left over cake?" He grinned, popping his head around the door.

"Twisted my arm," I said a little too loudly. Our energy connected, as always, we bounced off each other. Like we were kids again. I ran after him, knowing I wouldn't beat him to the kitchen, the adrenalin rush was worth running into him as he jumped out from the other side of the door. Laughter filled the house for the first time in a while.

The cake melted in my mouth; I savoured the velvety caramel chocolate taste, which combined with the raspberries I found in my freezer, was amazing.

"So, last night. Steve, the Firey, thinks the fire was deliberate. The Wills were lucky the shed and the house didn't blow up, with all the oils and other chemicals he has in that shed." Seamus paused to eat another scoop of dessert cake.

"They were lucky you were here. I saw what you did. I don't mean alerting them to the trouble. You held that fire from spreading any more, didn't you?" Another thing I hadn't paid close enough attention to – my friend's skills and those of the other powered people in the community. Instead of thinking our powers were trouble, I should've known they could also heal.

"Yeah, that was me. My powers have been increasing as much as yours." He shrugged. "I don't question it. I'm just pleased I can help people."

We ate the rest of our cake in silence.

"I was texting Mike. That last blackout wasn't the teenagers he was working with. Jon and Steve agree it was something to do with heat and chemicals, but as to whether it was a powered person or just an ordinary troublemaker, well the jury is still out on that."

I agreed with Seamus. There were several fronts we needed to attack if we were going to solve this mystery. "What are we going to do first? Re-read the paperwork, or watch the video again? Although I'm in two minds about whether I want to see Dad's face again just yet."

"I know what you mean." He reached across the table and gave my hand a squeeze. The energy leapt between us, like sticking a fork in a power point, but in a good way. "Did we read the documents on the thumb drive?"

I stuck the drive back into my laptop. I'd hidden it in the bottom of my slipper overnight. The family tree folder confirmed that version of the tree with the male line, including Jacob. A lump stuck in my throat. Dad's comment that they hadn't lied, but just kept the truth from me, sounded hollow, with what I now knew about my extended family.

"Now this is interesting." Seamus pointed to the name on the application to develop the Wynyard Street shops. *Dean Collier.*

"Wasn't that the name of the person trying to convince everyone that I'm trying to con the people of Spirit Town?" That knot in the pit of my stomach that had nothing to do with the food I ate tightened a notch.

"Yes." Seamus leant closer to the screen, making the image bigger and examining the bottom, where the time and date stamp sat alongside the signature.

"So how do we prove that the form with Dean Collier's signature is the true copy? We'd would need more evidence than the council time date seal surely." A glimmer of hope lifted my spirit.

"First, let's figure out who Dean Collier is. Why is he trying to discredit you? If you focus on that, I'll alert the others that there is an anomaly with the form. It's a shame the documents don't have to be lodged anywhere else, an official register or something." I could tell Seamus was thinking through all the possibilities.

"Wait! There might be." That glimmer of hope was growing. "Makayla is super-efficient; she has ideas on how to make a lot of the processes more effective. Max never let her set up anything. We had a chat and I'm planning to give her approval to make the changes." I turned the laptop towards me and looked up my emails. Luckily, Makayla had included my personal email when she sent out the list of items, she thought would make the place run smoother. I scrolled through her list. "Ah ha! See I was right. Thank you, Makayla! She's been keeping a register on our document management system. All the applications since she started her job, that's over two years now. I'll send the link to you. When you get to work can you confirm which version of the application is on record? Fingers crossed it's this one and not mine." I suspected that Dean was using smoke and mirrors to muddle the issue.

"I think we have a plan in place that just might work." Seamus looked at me.

"Maybe," I acknowledged grudgingly, not wanting to get too excited in case it all fell apart. "Thank so much for staying and helping."

"Not a problem. I'm always happy to help when there's cake involved," he quipped. "What time are the others coming?"

"Five." I looked at the time on the laptop. "It's four. Time for a shower first."

"Thanks, but I'll pass." He grinned. "I guess you won't mind if I heat up some left over Chinese?"

"I don't mind at all. Make yourself at home."

IZZIE ARRIVED EARLY. She knew I was an early riser and so she never worried she might wake me. She raised an eyebrow when she saw Seamus making the coffees, but all she said was "Morning all, I only came here for Spark cuddles."

Jon, Lexi and Lara arrived within a few minutes of each other. Seamus had coffee, tea and cake set up at the kitchen table. I'd spread the papers out on the dining table, including a copy of the key documents from the thumb drive.

"I know you guys are busy. I'm guessing the confrontation at the supermarket made its way to social media." Lara and Lexi exchanged looks that confirmed my guess. "I'm okay." The disbelief evident on Izzie's face.

"I'll admit I didn't handle it well," I conceded. "I'll be more prepared next time." I had the distinct feeling that next time would be soon.

"The good news is, we think we have figured out a way to prove Beth hasn't done anything wrong." Seamus' voice was strong, confident.

"There's a whole heap of information, some false, red herrings. We think we've discovered a way to tell what's truth and what's lies," I added, unable to contain my excitement. Working closely with Seamus boosted my energy. All my favourite people in one room, and Spark. Gratitude filled my thoughts.

"I hate to burst your bubble friend, but someone is loudly calling you all sorts of names. I want to get you on the radio to refute it all when you're ready," Izzie said firmly, taking a second piece of cake.

"There's been so many locals emailing, and ringing the office, offering you support," Lexi added, as she filled the kettle for another round of drinks. "I've kept a record of all the messages for you."

Lara joined Spark on the kitchen floor, shaking a ball of wool, as he chased it. "Do you need anything from me specifically? If the documents were lodged electronically, I may be able to confirm their authenticity." I wasn't yet used to Lara's skills with technology.

"Maybe." I considered the question. "If you can work with Lexi on that, she has a copy of all the documents, except these." I passed a copy of the documents from the thumb drive to Lexi.

"Changing the subject, the fire last night was deliberate," Jon said. "Across the road. No one was hurt," he added, before Lexi, Lara or Izzie had a chance to ask any questions. "Fred and I'll be busy with Mike, working out a more effective way of figuring out if crimes are deliberate acts, accidental side effects of a magic spell gone wrong, or deliberate acts by powered people. Even if we can identify the accidental acts, that's better than we have currently." Jon patted me on the back as he pushed his chair back and stood. "I know I don't have to say it but be careful."

I appreciated the gesture. "I will. I'll try to stay out of trouble too, though it seems to keep finding me these days."

Izzie followed Jon to the door. "Keep me updated, I want you on the radio as soon as you can." She gave me a hug. "I'll work with Lexi too. We'll sort it out."

"What if the intent of all this is to scare me, intimidate me, maybe cause me to choose to run back to the city? Problem is, they don't know me well enough. I'm stubborn," I mused.

"You don't say." Seamus chuckled. "They picked on the wrong person."

"The first step is to verify the documents on the thumb drive. I think all the other versions are red herrings, smoke and mirrors. Given to me to confuse me and keep me occupied." My head was clear for the first time since I was confronted at the office.

"Are the video and documents from the thumb drive enough evidence for the police to act?" Lara asked quietly, eyes wide like one of those soft toys that were popular a few years ago. "I mean it's just one person's opinion, someone who you can't question, and if legal documents can be forged, would a statutory declaration carry any weight legally?"

Jon rubbed his forehead wearily. "We can question the people Beth's dad named in the video. The additional documents will help. I'll have to check with our fraud squad."

Chapter 15

I drank my third coffee for the morning engulfed in the silence permeating the kitchen. Disquieting, seeing as I normally enjoy my own company. Hot tears filled my eyes, I let them travel down my cheek. Why was I missing my friends who only walked out the door a few minutes ago? Memories of running through the house with Seamus, laughing as we played at whatever mischief we were up to. Meals with my parents, and Grandma. All distant memories, threatening to fade with the increasing passage of time.

"Why didn't I pay more attention to what was going on around me?"

Spark mewed.

I bent to pick him up and he leapt into my arms.

My despair dissolved at the touch of his paw on my arm. A glimmer of hope, a lightbulb in my brain. Family was important, and my friends had my back too.

"There's no time for sorrow or sadness; there's work to be done."

The little ball of fluff purred loudly, agreeing with me.

Family was still a puzzle to me, but one I'd sort in due course. My friends had it covered. My task was to conduct more investigation and preparation for my meeting with council. "Or we could go and get some furniture for my office."

Spark climbed up onto my shoulder, nuzzling my neck. This bond between human and familiar, unlike any other experience. I understood what people meant by *my spirit soars* because with Spark my spirit did soar. My heart filled with joy I didn't know was possible. My energy buzzed, vibrating at a high frequency.

I sent a text to the five who had lifted my spirits; I knew they were all worried about me.

Shopping for home office furniture in Apple Tree. Message if I need to be at any meetings. I'll text when I'm home.

I didn't feel like running into anyone who was likely to ask me about being mayor, or to clarify the development applications, and while the nearest town was only ten minutes by car it would be easier for me to choose a desk lamp without being recognised.

"That's the plan, anyway," I told Buddy, patting him after listening to him devour an apple.

"What am I going to do with you?" Spark looked up at me, ready by the front door when I exited my room after changing into floral pants, a black shirt, and a pink hoodie. My runners, in shades of blue, pink and purple, my favourite non workday shoes. If I needed to attend a meeting at council or anywhere else, it would only take a few minutes to come back and change into more appropriate clothing. I felt like I was back at high school, cutting the days classes. I grinned.

"I did plan on leaving you here, I mean I know you'll be safe and not destroy anything." I knew Spark had stressed the evening before when I was accosted in the supermarket. Not that he could've saved me from that altercation, we were both happier with him in the car.

"There'll still be days when you'll stay home alone. After we clean up this mess." Our connection, difficult to describe, was stronger than any bond I'd experienced, even with my best friend. I lifted him onto the back seat, and he put himself in the carrier. I only locked it for safety, in case we were ever in an accident. I knew he would never leave the carrier while I was driving anywhere.

I'd forgotten how much bigger Apple Tree was than Spirit Town. The street buzzed with people. At 8:30 in the morning, school or work were the likely destinations for most of the traffic. I found a car park at the back of the furniture store.

"I won't be long," I informed a purring Spark, all curled up snoozing after the early morning household full of people.

"Ugg. No wonder the car park had so many vacant spaces." The sign on the door advised the shop didn't open until nine in the morning. Luckily the café next door was open. I could sit at an outside table and make sure the car was okay. I didn't think anyone would try to hurt my familiar, I'd left the windows open a little to give him air. If the café hadn't been in such a good position, I would have grabbed takeaway and eaten it in the car.

My energy was bubbling along, enjoying the anonymity. The young lass behind the counter, with her long black hair braided up into a bun, probably fifteen years my junior. She smiled as she asked for my order. The *Positive Vibes* café was living up to its name.

People watching was an activity I used to engage in when I lived in the city. The café walls were black, wainscoting, with local artist paintings adding to the ambience. A sign on the counter advised the café workers were all young people learning hospitality skills, a community initiative. The three staff I could see, dressed in black. Hair tied back. Friendly, smiling, cheerful, courteous. Customers dressed in work clothes, black trousers and dress shirts, probably admin or businesses of some kind. Calling in for a cuppa to keep them going until lunch. I knew the routine well; it reminded me of my time in the city.

The young lady with her red hair tied back into a bun smiled as she placed my takeaway mug of mocha and plate with a small piece of chocolate brownie on the table.

"Yum, thank you. I love the energy and the atmosphere in your café." I smiled at her.

"You are welcome." She beamed. "My aunt is one of the people in the committee that started this initiative." I watched her almost skip back through the door, to share the positive comment. The brownie was one of those melt-in-your-mouth desserts that I wished I had learnt how to make.

Practise, practise, practise!

Grandma's voice echoed in my brain. Maybe, after all this, I'd find time for learning new skills, or practising those recipes grandma taught me so long ago.

A movement near my car caught my attention. I couldn't see anyone. Curious, I popped the rest of the brownie in my mouth, picked up my mocha and headed over. Spark was still sound asleep, curled up in a ball. I caught another movement, just outside my vision.

Ah

Intuition told me it was a spirit, a magical movement most people wouldn't pay any attention to.

Jacob? Or something more malevolent?

I didn't get the sense of danger. I wasn't going to turn around and go home without at least looking some furniture for the dining room, er office.

Protection over the car and my familiar.

I waved my arm over the vehicle, setting my intention for safety for Spark. My fingers vibrated as the energy transferred to the space around the car, creating a shield. I could see the shimmering energy, but others wouldn't see it, unless they were specifically seeking it. A sense of calm permeated.

I walked tall into the shop as soon as the disinterested gentleman unlocked the glass sliding doors. The name tag on his bright yellow shirt told me his name was Chris. I smiled at him, but he was staring straight ahead, probably wishing he was at home playing video games.

The lighting section was straight in front of me, with an ordinary looking desk lamp on special, almost identical to mine when I swotted for my year twelve exams. Fifteen dollars according to the sign on the shelf. Bonus. I tucked it under my left arm and headed for the furniture.

Flat packs weren't my favourite furniture option, but they were easier to slot into the back of my car. I chose the wood laminate look, rather than stark white. The bookshelf a little taller than me was the best option. Anything bigger would be too difficult to carry. I hadn't seen any trolleys when I arrived, so I took a photo of the ticket on the assembled bookshelf. A cute little table, with the matching laminate, might come in handy. I snapped a photo of its ticket. One desk, same material, the shelves on top were a bonus. I dreaded to think how long it would take me to assemble my office furniture, but I needed organisation and control in my life.

The one cashier operating at the front of the store was flushed. Flustered. Customers in front of me, all with baskets of office stationery, tins of coffee, tea bags, sugar sachets, serviettes, pens, note pads, post it notes and assorted bits and pieces. I couldn't see their faces, but each gave off an air of frustration; *hurry up and serve me, I have work to do*. Guessing people's stories amused me.

"You're a long way from home, Miss Mayor," sneered a familiar voice I tried my best to ignore. If I left now, I'd have to return to buy my furniture later. I didn't give in to bullies. Not without a fight. My hackles were up. The prickly sensation on the back of my neck. I didn't want to turn around, but if I didn't, he'd continue to speak, loudly, to draw attention. His aim was to cause as much trouble as possible.

"Just doing a bit of shopping," I said brightly. "I see you've been stocking up on office supplies too." His basket was empty except for a packet of pens and a notebook. Why didn't he just carry them? Nothing there to use as a distraction.

"I'm renting an office locally. That's none of your concern." His eyes scanned the area, specifically those in line, close enough to hear him. "Have you managed to make headway with solving your current dilemma? I thought you'd be meeting with council, trying to convince them you aren't corrupt." His voice got louder as he reached the end of his sentence. A few of the people turned to look at us. I'd only moved forward one place in the queue. The person behind the counter was in no hurry complete customer transactions.

I sighed. No choice but to contain this conversation as best I could, to turn the tables on my detractor. I reached into my bag and found my phone. As I took out my business card, I snapped a couple of photos of the man. If challenged, I could show photographs of the products on my list to purchase for the office.

"In case you've misplaced the card I gave you yesterday, here's another one. As I explained yesterday, if you'd like to email or ring my office, we can arrange a meeting to discuss your concerns." My heart was thumping so loudly. I didn't mention the town meeting, he didn't need a wider audience to play up to. I steeled my mind. Putting up the wall to stop him reading my mind. I sent vibes willing the checkout person to work faster.

A second cashier hurried over to the front counter.

The sound of a mobile beeping turned the heads of those closest to me. It was his mobile, beeping shrilly like a fire alarm. Impeccable timing. My protagonist left the line up to talk to, or rather listen to whoever was on the other end of the line.

"Can I help you?" The shop assistant was about my age, wearing the signature yellow shirt and bright blue pants.

"Yes, thanks, I'd like to buy this lamp." I placed the lamp on the counter. "And these items." I showed him the photos I had taken.

"There's a fee if you need them delivered," The sandy haired guy named Ben, according to his shirt, told me, fingers poised on the tablet in front of him.

"Thanks, but I think they'll fit in my car, if I lay the back seat down," I responded.

"Drive round the back to the loading dock and pick up the items." He handed me the receipt.

I exited the building without a backward glance, reaching my car, hopefully before anyone else left the furniture store. I put the lamp on the floor in the front passenger seat and followed the road around to the loading dock.

My heart rate slackened off as I drove away. I concentrated on my breathing. Not many people paid attention to the conversation; I convinced myself it was a non-event. The man, I suspected it was probably the Dean Collier who Seamus had mentioned, was just trying to cause trouble. Had he followed me or was it a coincidence?

"Come on, little guy." Thankfully, with some manoeuvring the carrier fitted on one side of the back seat. I pushed the other side flat and tilted the front passenger seat as far forward as possible. Fingers crossed that the packages would fit, I handed my receipt to the person who came to the roller door. He eyed my little car doubtfully.

"They should fit," I said with as much cheer as I could muster.

He returned with a trolley with three longish boxes.

"Where there's a will there's a way," I told him determinedly.

A few minutes later I'd managed to shut the back door of the car. There was a tiny gap between the back door and the largest box. It rested on the glove box. The storeman shook his head as he pushed the trolley back through the roller door.

As I drove towards the exit, I noticed the well-dressed man watching me. He was standing beside a smart looking black car. Not a sports car, but an executive sedan, like something our previous mayor would have driven. My sedan, or rather my parents' old car, wasn't flash or new, but it was good enough for me. It was blue, and probably needed a service. I'd add that to my list of things to get onto once things settled.

FLAT PACKS WEREN'T my favourite way to spend the morning.

My mobile rang as I was struggling the largest box into the dining room. It clunked to the ground, missing Spark who was investigating the mess. I missed the call. I'd promised to let everyone know I was back home, so I sent a group text. The missed call was from a number I didn't recognise. They could leave a message.

Five beeps in quick succession.

Six.

I eyed the boxes laid out across the floor.

Seven.

I harrumphed and stood up from my kneeling position. Spark padded across the boxes, checking out our purchases. I was tempted to send a group text asking who would like to help me assemble some furniture. I read through my texts.

Lara sent a smiley face.

Lexi sent a thumbs up.

There wasn't a text from Jon but then I expected he would be busy.

We can fit in a radio interview tomorrow if you are up for it. – Izzie.

Extraordinary council meeting this afternoon at 3. – Seamus.

Watch your back, – Unknown Caller.

Dinner after council meeting – all meet at Evie's at 6? – Seamus.

I responded to Izzie and Seamus, and ignored the mysterious text that I assumed was from my stalker.

Fuelled by the frustration of not being able to do my job properly, little flecks of light zinged from my fingertips as I yanked the wood look melanite from the packaging. There was a flash of brown as an elf with a surprised expression pushed my hands out of the way.

"We're here to put this together for you, as long as you get out of the way," the little creature said sternly, as a second elf, his face puckered up in a frown, emerged from behind the second box. Spark sniffed both elves as they stood still for a few seconds. "So now are you satisfied?" The first elf said to my familiar. Spark sat at my feet, apparently unconcerned by our unexpected visitors.

"Thank you." I didn't know what else to say, so I retreated to the chair behind the dining table. "It'll give me a chance to read through the papers again," I told Spark as he climbed up on my lap.

It was fascinating to watch as the two little folk deftly lifted each piece, assembling them into the furniture I'd seen at the store. The bookshelf materialised as I watched, taking a fraction of the time as it would have taken me.

I must have dozed off because I was jarred awake by the beeping of my mobile phone.

Something was wrong. It was two in the afternoon, according to the clock and the light outside my window. Only it wasn't my window. Or my house. The wooden panels on the wall, the rug of rough red wool, thick and bristly looking, weren't familiar. I touched the fabric on the armchair I was slouched in. Prickly and orange. A matching chair sat opposite me. A roughly built wooden table, between the two. I stood up. Unsure whether to check out the other rooms in this cottage, or figure out where I was? A sound outside decided it for me.

A quick assessment of the room I found myself in revealed two options. Stay in the room without any hiding place, and potentially be discovered, or duck into one of the other rooms, hoping for a way out or at least a proper hiding spot. I slipped into the room on the other side of the only other door in the room as the front door opened. Two men strode in. Raised voices, it was easy to hear their conversation.

"We must keep this up. We can't have Beth stay on as mayor and figure out the real history of the community." The man's voice was angry, agitated.

The room I found myself in, a small kitchenette-laundry, not much bigger than my bathroom. Whoever lived here did not enjoy cooking. Good news – the external door was not locked. I tested the handle. An escape route. I held my breath. I wasn't ready to leave yet. My curiosity overrode my fear.

"Can't we all work together? I mean there aren't so many in the coven that we can afford to make enemies and keep killing people. With Beth gone, there are others who'll take on the role her family were charged to keep safe. We can't risk the hierarchy finding out what's happening here."

Now I was intrigued. There was something familiar about that voice. I couldn't place it, and I didn't feel brave enough to peek and get a visual of the two speakers. The kitchen bench didn't offer any weapon options. Opening drawers and cupboards, out of the question – too noisy.

"You're only saying that because of your family situation," Sneered voice one. "We could take more drastic measures. Spirit Town doesn't have to be a haven for gifted people. We could change their reality – no one would be any the wiser."

I shivered. I didn't understand the context, but I knew that voice. My antagonist from the shop. My instincts were torn. Stay and learn more or leave.

"I'll not support that move. If you insist on that course of action, I'll be reporting you. Not to Beth, to those much higher up." The stern tone of voice triggered a memory.

Jacob?

Anything was possible.

"This has gone on for long enough. Your family's personal vendetta with Beth's family, my family, ends now."

I heard foots steps striding towards where I stood. I watched in astonishment as the external door swung open. I didn't need any additional encouragement. I darted out the door, as a sharp beeping sound startled me.

It took a few seconds to realise I must've dozed off on the chair in the dining room, with my head on my laptop in the middle of the table. The alarm on my mobile reminded me to prepare for my afternoon's meeting.

With no sign of the tiny elves, their handy work was evident. Along one of the walls stood the tall bookshelf, ready and waiting to have books and knickknacks occupy its shelves. The smaller table sat just inside the doorway, exactly where I would've placed it. My desk was assembled and sitting to one side. It wouldn't take long to move it into position. Perfectly put together, I couldn't tell where the screws or dowel nails held them together. The elves did an amazing job. How long had they been part of the service and how did they get back to the shop? Likely an enchantment whisked them back as soon as their work was completed.

As I dozed, I'd eavesdropped on a conversation between Jacob and Dean Collier. If I heard correctly, they belonged to a coven, and worked together on projects, until now? Are covens a real thing and not just the stuff of fairy tales? There wasn't time to figure out if I'd stumbled on a real encounter, in less than an hour I was due to defend myself at council.

I checked the water level in the kettle and made a mug of coffee. While the water boiled, I quickly changed. Black suit. Red shirt. Power dressing. Shiny black boots. Hair pulled back tightly into a bun.

Twenty minutes left to finish preparation for the meeting.

My laptop bag contained my laptop, and relevant documents, the thumb drive safely tucked in the pocket of my pants.

Keep a clear head. Focus on the meeting. On the facts.

The muscles in my stomach clenched at the thought of relinquishing my mayoral role. But I was pragmatic. I wanted the best outcome for the village. If someone else identified a better option, I'd handover, job done. My focus this afternoon, to clear my name, took priority. I gulped my coffee, wanting to get to the council chambers in plenty of time.

"You're staying here, Spark." I expected a fuss, but my familiar looked at me from his bed in the corner of the kitchen. His expression one of resignation. "You have food, water, and your toys. I won't be late."

I placed my invisible cloak of protection around my shoulders. Its velvety purple material was comforting. A trick learnt from my grandma a long time ago, to protect me from the school yard teasing that came with growing up in a town with ordinary and extraordinary people. "If I can cloak myself, surely I can cloak the house." Spark stood, stretched and turned in a circle the way cats do when they are settling in for a nap. "Thanks, Spark." I spun slowly in a circle, clockwise and chanted,

"By the power of the north, the south, the east, and the west, I call the spirits of my ancestors to protect our home, the animals and humans who live here or who are invited guests. Earth, water, air, fire and spirit, I ask the elements to ensure the safety of all who I love and care for." I hesitated, not sure how to end my chant. I recalled a phrase from long ago. *"This I ask, so mote it be."*

Chapter 16

I arrived at the council chambers fifteen minutes early. Surprised to find the room already occupied by the five councillors, I took a step backwards and closed the door. I guess I should've knocked first.

I hesitated. The door opened while I was wondering what to do while I waited.

"We'll be about ten minutes," Jamie said quietly but firmly. "If you could please wait in the reception area." Before I could reply, he disappeared behind the closed door.

I'd never been called in front of the principal's office, but this is how I imagined it. The fizzing of my energy building up as my stubbornness kicked in. The sound of the front door banging open, or shut, piqued my curiosity. Especially as it was followed by Makayla's voice. "Oh, my goodness."

"Hi Makayla." I spoke as I walked into reception, trying not to startle her. Kneeling on the floor, she collected loose papers into a pile. "Do you need some help?" I picked up a couple of stray pieces.

"Thanks, Beth." I'd insisted she call me by my name rather than Miss Mayor. I noticed the tiny hesitation as she got used to using my first name. "A random wind blew the door open and shut. I'd just arranged these in order for Jamie's afternoon meeting." If she knew the intent of the meeting, she didn't let on. Her expression conveyed she was pleased to see me. It wasn't likely she'd know the details of councillor meetings, unless she needed to prepare materials.

"Do you want some help sorting them back into order?" I've some time before my meeting." It was likely my emotions produced the random breeze, assisting to rectify it the least I could do.

"Thank you! I'd appreciate it. Jamie wants six bundles of these. Ten pages in each bundle. Whoever sent them has cloaked them in a spell, so that only those who are required to can read the details. The pages are numbered, which makes sorting them into piles easy." She sat back on her haunches. "Did that make sense?"

"Perfect sense," I said as I quickly sorted the pages, while she watched, eyes wide. Not only could I see the words on the pages clearly, the cloaking didn't work for me, but each page almost flew from my fingers to the right pile. "It appears the enchantment is sorting them." I assumed she knew I possessed certain gifts. "I tend not to use my skills at work. Sometimes it happens without me meaning to," I offered by way of explanation.

"Mine is drawing," Makayla said quietly. "I can draw anything or anyone. I have so many drawings at home. When I save enough money, I want to travel and maybe sell my drawings. My parents say that's not a proper job."

"It could be a proper job. I write words, and as a journalist, I get money for writing. You could illustrate books, or comics, or cards, the possibilities are endless." I was passionate about this. "If you enjoy it that is." I handed her the six piles of papers, all sorted and ready for Jamie. Before I could mention her email about efficiencies in the office, which I'd loved and wanted to talk to her about, Jamie entered the reception area.

Makayla slipped each pile into a manilla folder, handing the folders to Jamie.

"Beth." He nodded to me. "Please join us now." Eyes straight ahead, I followed Jamie, hoping to get back to say goodbye to Makayla when the meeting finished.

Seated around the table were Drew, Seamus, Greg, Kim and the man from the confrontations that I took to be Dean, Jamie sat and motioned for me sit on the opposite side of the table, so I'd be facing them. Like an inquisition.

I nodded at each person as I took my seat at the table. With slow deliberate movements I unpacked my laptop bag. My laptop first, then the papers. All eyes were on me as I organised the documents. They could wait while I calmed my breathing. Raising the wall to block my mind being read by Dean or anyone else was the last step. Not sure if this would block Seamus, I intentionally didn't try to connect with him. Finally, I laid the thumb drive on the table next to my laptop. Only after taking a drink from my metal water bottle did I look up. "Good afternoon, Jamie, Seamus, Drew, Greg, Kim, and Dean." I considered shaking hands but decided against it. I looked each person, in the eye, including Dean.

"I didn't realise you knew Dean," Jamie spoke first. I didn't bother explaining that Dean was a bully. I let it lie, for now. "You're aware that Dean has raised concerns about recent development applications, which may negatively impact our town." He passed a folder to each person at the table, keeping one for himself. "These documents speak for themselves. I'll give everyone a chance to read them."

I didn't open my folder.

Instead, I handed out the documents from the thumb drive. "When you've read those documents, you need to review these, the true copies, as ratified by our council records management system." I didn't name anyone. "I investigated Dean's claims, as I imagine you would, if you were accused of something you didn't do. There is no record on council or at any office, of development applications submitted by me. What there is, clearly documented, are several development applications submitted by a company owned by Dean Collier. After what happened when our previous mayor had tried to pass some applications without due diligence, the previous deputy mayor worked with the police and the neighbouring councils on a process whereby any applications had to be ratified by three separate processes, none of which are controlled by me, or anyone on council. An accountability precaution." I laid my hands in front of my laptop. Holding the gaze of each person sitting opposite me. "If you call in an independent auditor from the city, they'll confirm what I've just told you."

I directed the next part to Jamie. "I trust that would be the next step, to ascertain the truth of the situation. I don't want to be seen to sway you either way, so I won't suggest the best auditor." I stopped, referring to the notes on my laptop. I didn't need to, but it gave me a moment to assess the room. No one interjected, which I took as a good sign. "Friday afternoon at four in the afternoon, we'll hold the town meeting, in the high school auditorium. To address the questions raised to me, and about me. Please ask Makayla to set that up, and to liaise with the newspaper and the local radio station to make sure the message gets out." I lowered my gaze to check my notes once more. I typed in a few notes, for my own reference, and honestly to assert my authority.

This time I addressed the other councillors. They'd read through the documents I'd handed them and were now watching me "Do you need any further information from me? Have I provided sufficient evidence to refute the malicious claims levelled against me?" Drew, Kim and Jamie lowered their gaze. Seamus contained the smile I saw in his eyes. I didn't bother acknowledging Dean. He didn't belong in the council and so there was no need to.

Greg glanced around at the others seated on that side of the table. He sighed, tried to stop it, but it was too late, I caught it. I'd won. He leant forward a little. I knew it was a trick to get someone on side. It wouldn't work for me, he slumped back in his seat and turned to Jamie. I almost felt sorry for him.

Jamie turned away from Greg, addressing me directly, "As soon as we leave this room, I'll get Makayla to pull all the development applications dated in the last twelve months, from the files. I'll compare it to what I have here." His gesture included all the papers strewn across in front of him. "It might take a few days to organise the audit. It'll be more efficient if you work directly with Makayla on what you need for the town meeting." Jamie turned to Dean. "It's best if you leave now, Dean. I'll be in touch if the auditor needs any information from you, otherwise thank you for raising your concerns." He stood up, and held open the door for Dean, shutting it firmly after him. Dean didn't speak, his darkness lingered after the door closed behind him. I made a note to bring incense and cleanse the room, or preferably the whole building.

"Beth. Informally, I apologise for any inconvenience. You stepped aside, pending this meeting, thank you for your time and patience. I want to have a quick word with the others. I'll ring you afterwards." I knew that was code for *I don't know whether to ask you to come back to work or not.*

"I appreciate the position you've been put in." It was one of the reasons I didn't ask Seamus to step in, in my absence. It took a few seconds to gather my papers and laptop back into my bag. The thumb drive, I tucked back into the pocket of my trousers. "I'll speak to Makayla about Friday's meeting." I hesitated for a couple of seconds. "The results of the audit will assure you I'd nothing to do with those applications. I advise not approving any applications of Dean's, until you investigate him further. His motives aren't in the best interests of our town." I left it there and nodded to the others seated around the table. Seamus' words *good job* echoed as I shut the door quietly behind me.

"Is everything okay?" Makayla greeted me, her face betrayed her concern. "That Mr Collier strode out of here, leaving such a foul energy behind. I swept it out with the magic broom I drew." She pointed to a drawing of a broom lying against the wall. "I may have forgotten to mention that what I draw comes to life."

"Now that's cool," I told her, and I meant it. "Yes, everything is okay. Mr Collier didn't get the results he was hoping for. I'd suggest drawing and lighting some incense and candles to cleanse the space, once that meeting finishes." I wasn't sure exactly what he was hoping for apart from discrediting me and making me resign, but I was glad Makayla had swept away his energy. The residue was enough to make me gag. "If you have time, I'd like some help arranging a town meeting on Friday."

Makayla motioned for me to sit. I pulled the chair over to her desk and opened my laptop.

"I've sent you an email with the details." I pressed send on one I'd drafted earlier. "If you can get the school hall, after school on Friday, and liaise with Lexi and Izzie to get the word out. I'll email the townsfolk who sent me questions ..."

The shrill tone of the telephone on Makayla's desk interrupted us. My mobile, on silent, I'd missed a call and two messages, from an unknown caller.

You haven't won yet. Watch your back.

Chapter 17

The menacing note on my windscreen, written in black paint *You haven't won yet* was even more unsettling.

"Hi, Lexi, I hate to ask, but can you please drive me home, now? I'm worried about Spark. He's been home for a couple of hours now. Sorry, I know it's early and I wouldn't ask unless I had to." I felt a little silly bursting in like that. I could've walked and been home in less than thirty minutes.

"Sure thing." Without asking any questions, Lexi led me out to where her car was parked, not far from mine. "Isn't that your—" Lexi's voice faded. "Oh, I see, come on, get in."

"Thanks. I'm just going to give Jon a quick ring." I hopped into Lexi's Beetle. The cutest car ever, sky blue with orange racing stripes.

"Go right ahead. We'll be there in a jiffy." Lexi deftly swung the car around and pointed it towards home.

I got Jon's answering service, rather than ring the station, I left a message. "Hi, Jon, it's Beth. I hate to ask but can you or Fred check my car, in the car park behind the office, it's got black paint on it, a threat. I don't know if you can fingerprint it. I'll be at home, thanks." I tucked my phone into my bag as Lexi pulled up out the front.

"I'll come in with you. To see Spark." She wasn't fooling me; I knew she didn't want me to go to in alone.

"I wouldn't have it any other way." I found myself grinning. The text and the note had scared me a little, but my stubbornness kicked in.

"Um, Beth, there's someone sitting on your verandah." Lexi's voice sounded a little reticent. "Do you know him?"

I looked to where a man about my age, was sitting on a wicker chair. His dark hair and jeans gave him away. "Jacob," I said loudly, in a not unfriendly voice. I felt Lexi's puzzled expression from behind me as I blocked her way in case, he wasn't friendly after all.

"You're a hard person to find, cousin." He strode over and gave me a quick hug. "This must be Lexi. You've spoken so much about her." He smiled and shook her hand.

"Your cousin Jacob?" Lexi said. I knew I'd never mentioned him except in the brief discussion that morning.

"Let's get in out of the cold." I fumbled for the keys and was greeted at the door by a fluffy ball of fur landing on me.

"I've always preferred dogs myself. Less, fluffy." he said with only a hint of sarcasm. I'd the feeling he had already been inside and met Spark, who was more interested in Lexi, who always spoiled him. Jacob followed me as I filled the kettle. "I hear you won round one," he said quietly. "Dean has gone. He's conceded you're more on the ball than he thought. 'A force to be reckoned with' were his words. He'll spend time licking his wounds, garnering support, but he will be back."

"Is he related to us?" I asked the question that had been worrying me, since that last dream interaction.

"To me, yes, not you. It's complicated. I'm the link to you both. That's all I can say for now."

"Coffee?"

Jacob nodded. I knew Lexi would have one as well.

"Are the time slips linked to Dean, and the power outages? Or are they teenage experimentation?

"Dean got into their heads. The teens think they caused it all, but Dean was behind it all. Now that he's gone, you or I can close the time slips, unless you want to keep visiting your grandma?" Something about the way Jacob spoke made my stomach flip flop. It was tempting to keep the time slip open, to catch a glimpse of Grandma's life, when she was younger. That was selfish, and not the sort of thing I could do in good conscience, even if I wasn't mayor.

"Why was Dean here, and you, why now? Not that I mind meeting family."

"Your powers. For years you chose to ignore them. In a short space of time, you chose to become mayor and your magic is growing strong. More so each day. You have become a threat to Dean and those like him. His aim was to discredit you, as mayor and in case you chose to take on the role vacated by your mother."

I understood what Jacob meant, still, it was a lot to take in.

Lexi joined the table, with Spark on her shoulder. She sipped her coffee, glancing at me and Jacob.

"It's okay, Lexi, I'm safe, you don't have to stay. Seamus will be here soon, and Jon too." It was true, and while I didn't think Jacob a threat, it did not harm to remind him that others were looking out for me too.

Lexi smiled gratefully. "I do have family commitments." The absolute truth. "I'll see you tomorrow." She handed Spark to me and left.

I eyed my cousin. Less imposing in person, now that we were standing together in my home and not in a dream state.

"I know you have questions. I live a long way away, but I move between worlds. I am part of the coven with Dean, and many others. Our coven is meant to keep the natural order of things, and not get involved in power plays. If he returns to the coven he will receive a punishment." Jacob took a sip of the coffee I'd made for him. I smiled, until that point, I still wasn't entirely sure he was real, in the same form as Lexi or me.

"You want to continue on as mayor?"

I considered the question. "I think so. Unless there's someone more suited."

"What about the role of judge?" Jacob's face was expressionless, he could have been asking about the weather.

"I don't know." Which was true. I hadn't given it any thought.

"Agnes seems to think you need more time to grow into the role. That's what she advised my bosses. They are willing to give her time to train you. One whole cycle, that's a year of the seasons."

As I heard the words, images formed in front of my eyes. A ceremony with Boris and Trudie presiding. Many familiar faces in the crowd. I blinked; the image disappeared. "Are Trudie and Boris leaders of your coven?" Slowly, things were beginning to make sense.

"Yes. You're a quick study. If you have any other questions, I'll be around for a couple of days."

"And after that?" There were so many questions spinning in my brain, and I didn't know if I'd have the opportunity to talk to them all before my cousin returned to wherever he came from.

"You'll figure it out." I looked up, as Jacob faded. If I hadn't witnessed it, I wouldn't have believed it possible.

Chapter 18

The banging open of my front door brought me out of my trance.

"Are you okay?" Seamus hugged me, then held me at arm's length, frowning as he assessed my energy levels.

"I'm fine, honestly." I turned as Jon and Lara walked in behind Seamus. "Did I forget we were meeting this afternoon?"

"I checked the damage to your car. Fred's washing off the paint and he'll drop your car home later." Jon held his pen, poised over his notepad. "Do you have any idea who vandalised your car? I don't have spare resources to watch your house." He looked crestfallen.

I reached out my hand, and gently touched his arm. "Please, everyone, sit down. I'm okay, honestly. Jacob has filled me in on some details. The person behind most of what has been happening, his name is Dean Collier." Jon scribbled in his notebook, and Seamus stood up, a thunderous look on his face. "Dean's gone. Apparently, I was too much of a threat. He'll be back one day, but we'll be prepared. I'll be prepared."

"Why does he want to harm you?" Lara whispered; she fingers were playing with her car keys. I touched her hand, her fingers slowed and stopped.

"It's complicated. A story for over a long leisurely meal sometime. The important thing now is we are safe, the threat has gone, and things can go back to normal." I filled the kettle with water, on the off chance anyone wanted a cuppa.

Spark chose that precise moment to pounce on the ball of wool next to his bed. We laughed, as the ball slipped through his paws, landing on Seamus's shoe. He bent, throwing the ball back to the kitten's bed. "Did I hear you mention a meal? I wouldn't say no to a hearty pumpkin soup and crusty bread. I have it on good authority that's the special at the café tonight."

MAYBE I SHOULD'VE LET Seamus stay the night. I'd shooed him away, when he dropped me home after dinner, assuring him I'd be fine. Each time I closed my eyes, I found myself chased by Dean, and a mob of angry people I didn't know. A timeslip, or my overactive imagination? The almost full moon peeked from behind some clouds, creating an eerie backdrop as I opened the front door. The cold night air hit my cheeks; the blanket I'd dragged from Grandma's bed kept the rest of my body warm.

I yearned to visit with my parents, and Grandma, just once more. I'd ask all the questions currently running around in my brain. I'd apologise first, for ignoring my powers for so long.

A piece of paper fluttered onto the table. I looked up, as a Tawny Frogmouth flew over the roof, disappearing to the east. In the silence I heard the noise her wings made as they cut through the air. My fingers shook as I unfolded the paper.

Our darling daughter, we never meant to lie to you or keep secrets from you. Grandma made us promise to keep you safe. If you received this by owl, then you are interested in our heritage. Know that the three of us wished to be there for you during this time. We can connect in the dream world, during the in-between times and certain phases of the moon. We are with you always, never far away.

Agnes is watching over you for us, she can answer any questions you have. Embrace your past, and who you are, forgive those transgressions and keep safe always. You are destined for greatness, but it's your choice, don't let others sway you. We love you always x

"WE DECIDED ON FRIDAY next week for the town meeting. More time to ensure I've all the details and information on hand to refer to." Seamus had dragged me away from my desk on the pretext of an early lunch. The table in the conference room, bursting with sandwiches, coffees, and cakes. A round of applause had greeted me when Seamus led me in the door. Jon, Lara, Izzie, Lexi and Agnes each embraced me in turn.

Seamus handed me a takeaway cup with mocha written on the lid. "Greg, Jamie and the others have agreed you were set up, innocent of all charges so to speak. They wanted me to ask you to come back to work on Monday. If you want to continue as mayor."

I looked at Agnes. "I'd like to continue as mayor and explore my heritage." She nodded but didn't say a word. She didn't need to, we'd talk later. "Izzie, can I have spot on the radio this afternoon, or maybe Monday morning? I'll answer any questions you have." My old friend nodded.

Reaching for a sandwich, I sat between Lara and Seamus. I smiled at the faces around the table. I didn't have all the answers. I could've asked about the thefts, the wandering cattle, or the mysterious *Magic Shop*. But for the moment, it was enough, being here, with the people who meant the world to me. I felt the heat rise in my cheeks as under the table Seamus's hand reached for mine. The warmth as our fingers entwined radiated up my arm. Out of the corner of my eye, I noticed a pair of elves, dressed in shades of green and brown, giggling and pointing at me, from the corner behind the door. I smiled, no one else seem to notice them. They could wait, Seamus had put together this feast, and let's face it, we deserved five minutes to enjoy the calm before the storm.

The End.

Sarah Lewin

If you want to know more about me or my books, here are some details. Alternatively, please make contact via any of the social media listed below:

Email: sarahlewin@sarahlewin.com.au

You Tube: https://youtube.com/@sarahlewinangelwisdom539

Blog: https://sarahlewin.com

Facebook: https://www.facebook.com/SarahLewinAuthorWitchyMysteryBooks

Instagram: https://www.instagram.com/sarahlewin_author/

Amazon: https://amazon.com/author/sarahlewin

Goodreads: https://www.goodreads.com/author/show/43342156.Sarah_Lewin

Book Bub: https://www.bookbub.com/authors/sarah-lewin

My Witchy Mystery Books:

<u>Witch Wisdom Series:</u>

#1 – *Crone Wisdom*

#2 – *Ancient Wisdom*

#3 – *The Wisdom of the Witches* (available soon)

There are two free novella's in this series

The Coven

Kai's Story

<u>Spirit Town Cosy Mysteries:</u>

#1 – *Autumn Leaves Are Falling*

#2 – *Secrets Ghosts and Whispers*

<u>I also have a range of children's books available.</u>